Tacet Books

Ring Lardner

7 Best Short Stories

Edited by
August Nemo

Copyright© Tacet Books, 2022

All rights reserved.

Editor August Nemo
Cover and Interior Design Mayra Falcini
Marketing Horacio Corral

Dados Internacionais de Catalogação na Publicação (CIP)

Lardner, Ring.
L321   7 Best Short Stories / Ring Lardner – São Paulo, SP: Tacet Books, 2024.
237 p. : 14 x 21 cm

ISBN 978-65-89575-77-1

1. American literature. 2. Chronicles. 3. Short stories. I. Author.

CDD 810

Tacet Books

Made in silence

For noisy minds

www.tacetbooks.com

tacet.books@gmail.com

Table of Contents

The Author	5
Haircut	9
The Golden Honey Moon	27
My Roomy	55
Horseshoes	89
Harmony	127
Alibi Ike	157
Champion	187
Bonus content	219
Ring, by F. Scott Fitzgerald	219
Sport and play, by Ring Lardner	229
Discover Tacet Books	237

The Author

"It is no coincidence that the best of Mr. Lardner's stories are about games, for one may guess that Mr. Lardner's interest in games has solved one of the most difficult problems of the American writer; it has given him a clue, a centre, a meeting place for the diverse activities of people whom a vast continent isolates, whom no tradition controls. Game gives him what society gives his English brother."

Virginia Woolf

Ringgold Wilmer Lardner, commonly known as Ring Lardner,WW was an influential American sports columnist and short story writer, celebrated for his satirical takes on sports, marriage, and theater. Born on March 6, 1885, in Niles, Michigan, Lardner grew up as the youngest of nine children in a wealthy family. Despite disliking his given name, derived from a distant relative, he abbreviated it to Ring, which became the name he was known by throughout his career. His early years were marked by a passion for baseball, the stage, and music, and he later attended the Armour Institute in Chicago.

Lardner began his career as a sports columnist for the South Bend Times in 1905, quickly advancing to notable positions with the Inter-Ocean and the Chicago Examiner. His humorous baseball column, Pullman Pastimes, eventually led him to the Boston American and the Chicago Tribune, where his syndicated column, In the Wake of the News, gained widespread popularity. His work extended beyond sports, including dispatches from the World War I front, which were compiled in his book *My Four Weeks in France*. Lardner's sharp wit and keen observations made his writings resonate with readers, contributing to his legacy as a significant literary figure.

Lardner's first major literary success came in 1916 with the publication of *You Know Me Al*, an epistolary novel featuring letters from a fictional baseball player, Jack Keefe. The novel, initially published as short stories in *The Saturday Evening Post*, was praised for its use of vernacular and satire, earning admiration from contemporaries like Virginia Woolf and John O'Hara. Lardner continued to explore themes of sports and human nature in subsequent works, including *Treat 'Em Rough* and *The Real Dope*, cementing his reputation as a master storyteller with a unique voice.

In addition to his writing, Lardner had a deep interest in theater and music. He collaborated on Broadway productions, wrote skits for the Ziegfeld Follies, and composed songs with notable musicians. Despite his prolific output, Lardner held a modest view of his work, often underestimating its impact. However, his influence is evident in the works of Ernest Hemingway and F. Scott Fitzgerald, among others. Lardner's legacy endures through his innovative contributions to American literature and his insightful portrayal of early 20th-century American life

Haircut

I got another barber that comes over from Carterville and helps me out Saturdays, but the rest of the time I can get along all right alone. You can see for yourself that this ain't no New York City and besides that, the most of the boys works all day and don't have no leisure to drop in here and get themselves prettied up.

You're a newcomer, ain't you? I thought I hadn't seen you round before. I hope you like it good enough to stay. As I say, we ain't no New York City or Chicago, but we have pretty good times. Not as good, though, since Jim Kendall got killed. When he was alive, him and Hod Meyers used to keep this town in an uproar. I bet they was more laughin' done here than any town its size in America.

Jim was comical, and Hod was pretty near a match for him. Since Jim's gone, Hod tries to hold his end up just the same as ever, but it's tough goin' when you ain't got nobody to kind of work with.

They used to be plenty fun in here Saturdays. This place is jampacked Saturdays, from four o'clock on. Jim and Hod would show up right after their supper round six o'clock. Jim would set himself down in that big chair, nearest the blue spittoon. Whoever had been settin' in that chair, why they'd get up when Jim come in and at" it to him.

You'd of thought it was a reserved seat like they have sometimes in a theaytre. Hod would generally always stand or walk up and down or some Saturdays, of course, he'd be settin' in this chair part of the time, gettin' a haircut.

Well, Jim would set there a w'ile without opening his mouth only to spit, and then finally he'd say to me, "Whitey,"–my right name, that is, my right first name, is Dick, but everybody round here calls me Whitey– Jim would say, "Whitey, your nose looks like a rosebud tonight. You must of been drinkin' some of your aw de cologne."

So I'd say, "No, Jim, but you look like you'd been drinkin' something of that kind or somethin' worse."

Jim would have to laugh at that, but then he'd speak up and say, "No, I ain't had nothin' to drink, but that ain't sayin' I wouldn't like somethin'. I wouldn't even mind if it was wood alcohol."

Then Hod Meyers would say, "Neither would your wife." That would set everybody to laughin' because Jim and his wife wasn't on very good terms. She'd of divorced him only they wasn't no chance to get alimony and she didn't have no way to take care of herself and the kids. She couldn't never understand Jim. He was kind of rough, but a good fella at heart.

Him and Hod had all kinds of sport with Milt Sheppard. I don't suppose you've seen Milt. Well, he's got an Adam's apple that looks more like a mush-melon. So I'd be shavin' Milt and when I'd start to shave down here on his neck, Hod would holler, "Hey, Whitey, wait a minute! Before you cut into it, let's make up a pool and see who can guess closest to the number of seeds."

And Jim would say, "If Milt hadn't of been so hoggish, he'd of ordered a half a cantaloupe instead of a whole one and it might not of stuck in his throat."

All the boys would roar at this and Milt himself would force a smile, though the joke was on him. Jim certainly was a card!

There's his shavin' mug, setting on the shelf, right next to Charley Vail's. "Charles M. Vail." That's the druggist. He comes in regular for his shave, three times a week. And Jim's is the cup next to Charley's. "dames H. Kendall." Jim won't need no shavin' mug no more, but I'll leave it there just the same for old time's sake. Jim certainly was a character!

Years ago, Jim used to travel for a canned goods concern over in Carterville. They sold canned goods. Jim had the whole northern half of the State and was on the road five days out of every week. He'd drop in here Saturdays and tell his experiences for that week. It was rich.

I guess he paid more attention to playin' jokes than makin' sales. Finally the concern let him out and he come right home here and told everybody he'd been fired instead of sayin' he'd resigned like most fellas would of.

It was a Saturday and the shop was full and Jim got up out of that chair and says, "Gentlemen, I got an important announcement to make. I been fired from my job."

Well, they asked him if he was in earnest and he said he was and nobody could think of nothin' to say till Jim finally broke the ice himself. He says, "I been sellin' canned goods and now I'm canned goods myself."

You see, the concern he'd been workin' for was a factory that made canned goods. Over in Carterville. And now Jim said he was canned himself. He was certainly a card!

Jim had a great trick that he used to play w'ile he was travelin'. For instance, he'd be ridin' on a train and they'd come to some little town like, well, like, well, like, we'll say, like Benton. Jim would look out the train window and read the signs of the stores.

For instance, they'd be a sign, "Henry Smith, Dry Goods." Well, Jim would write down the name and the name of the town and when he got to wherever he was goin' he'd mail back a postal card to Henry Smith at Benton and not sign no name to it, but he'd write on the card, well somethin' like "Ask your wife about that book agent that spent the afternoon last week," or "Ask your Missus who kept her from gettin' lonesome the last time you was in Carterville." And he'd sign the card, "A Friend."

Of course, he never knew what really come of none of these jokes, but he could picture what probably happened and that was enough.

Jim didn't work very steady after he lost his position with the Carterville people. What he did earn, coin' odd jobs round town why he spent pretty near all of it on gin, and his family might of starved if the stores hadn't of carried them along. Jim's wife tried her hand at dressmakin', but they ain't nobody goin' to get rich makin' dresses in this town.

As I say, she'd of divorced Jim, only she seen that she couldn't support herself and the kids and she was always hopin' that some day Jim would cut out his habits and give her more than two or three dollars a week.

They was a time when she would go to whoever he was workin' for and ask them to give her his wages, but after she done this once or twice, he beat her to it by borrowin' most of his pay in advance. He told it all round town, how he had outfoxed his Missus. He certainly was a caution!

But he wasn't satisfied with just outwittin' her. He was sore the way she had acted, tryin' to grab off his pay. And he made up his mind he'd get even. Well, he waited till Evans's Circus was advertised to come to town. Then he told his wife and two kiddies that he was goin' to take them to the circus. The day of the circus, he told them he would get the tickets and meet them outside the entrance to the tent.

Well, he didn't have no intentions of bein' there or buyin' tickets or nothin'. He got full of gin and laid round Wright's poolroom all day. His wife and the kids waited and waited and of course he didn't show up. His wife didn't have a dime with her, or nowhere else, I guess. So she finally had to tell the kids it was all off and they cried like they wasn't never goin' to stop.

Well, it seems, w'ile they was cryin', Doc Stair come along and he asked what was the matter, but Mrs. Kendall was stubborn and wouldn't tell him, but the kids told him and he insisted on takin' them and their mother in the show. Jim found this out afterwards and it was one reason why he had it in for Doc Stair.

Doc Stair come here about a year and a half ago. He's a mighty handsome young fella and his clothes always look like he has them made to order. He goes to Detroit two or three times a year and w'ile he's there must have a tailor take his measure and then make him a suit to order. They cost pretty near twice as much, but they fit a whole lot better than if you just bought them in a store.

For a w'ile everybody was wonderin' why a young doctor like Doc Stair should come to a town like this where we already got old Doc Gamble and Doc Foote that's both been here for years and all the practice in town was always divided between the two of them.

Then they was a story got round that Doc Stair's gal had thronged him over, a gal up in the Northern Peninsula somewhere, and the reason he come here was to hide himself away and forget it. He said himself that he thought they wasn't nothin' like general practice in a place like ours to fit a man to be a good all round doctor. And that's why he'd came.

Anyways, it wasn't long before he was makin' enough to live on, though they tell me that he never dunned nobody for what they owed him, and the folks here certainly has got the owin' habit, even in my business. If I had all that was comin' to me for just shaves alone, I could go to Carterville and put up at the Mercer for a week and see a different picture every night. For instance, they's old George Purdy—but I guess I shouldn't ought to be gossipin'.

Well, last year, our coroner died, died of the flu. Ken Beatty, that was his name. He was the coroner. So they had to choose another man to be coroner in his place and they picked Doc Stair. He laughed at first and said he didn't want it, but they made him take it. It ain't no job that anybody would fight for and what a man makes out of it in a year would just about buy seeds for their garden. Doc's the kind, though, that can't say no to nothin' if you keep at him long enough.

But I was goin' to tell you about a poor boy we got here in town-Paul Dickson. He fell out of a tree when he was about ten years old. Lit on his head and it done somethin' to him and he ain't never been right. No harm in him, but just silly. Jim Kendall used to call him cuckoo; that's a name Jim had for anybody that was off their head, only he called people's head their bean. That was another of his gags, callin' head bean and callin' crazy people cuckoo. Only poor Paul ain't crazy, but just silly.

You can imagine that Jim used to have all kinds of fun with Paul. He'd send him to the White Front Garage for a left-handed monkey wrench. Of course they ain't no such thing as a left-handed monkey wrench.

And once we had a kind of a fair here and they was a baseball game between the fats and the leans and before the game started Jim called Paul over and sent him way down to Schrader's hardware store to get a key for the pitcher's box.

They wasn't nothin' in the way of gags that Jim couldn't think up, when he put his mind to it.

Poor Paul was always kind of suspicious of people, maybe on account of how Jim had kept foolin' him. Paul wouldn't have much to do with anybody only his own mother and Doc Stair and a girl here in town named Julie Gregg. That is, she ain't a girl no more, but pretty near thirty or over.

When Doc first come to town, Paul seemed to feel like here was a real friend and he hung round Doc's office most of the w'ile; the only time he wasn't there was when he'd go home to eat or sleep or when he seen Julie Gregg coin' her shoppin'.

When he looked out Doc's window and seen her, he'd run downstairs and join her and tag along with her to the different stores. The poor boy was crazy about Julie and she always treated him mighty nice and made him feel like he was welcome, though of course it wasn't nothin' but pity on her side.

Doc done all he could to improve Paul's mind and he told me once that he really thought the boy was getting better, that they was times when he was as bright and sensible as anybody else.

But I was goin' to tell you about Julie Gregg. Old man Gregg was in the lumber business, but got to drinkin' and lost the most of his money and when he died, he didn't leave nothin' but the house and just enough insurance for the girl to skimp along on.

Her mother was a kind of a half invalid and didn't hardly ever leave the house. Julie wanted to sell the place and move somewhere else after the old man died, but the mother said she was born here and would die here. It was tough on Julie as the young people round this town—well, she's too good for them.

She'd been away to school and Chicago and New York and different places and they ain't no subject she can't talk on, where you take the rest of the young folks here and you mention anything to them outside of Gloria Swanson or Tommy Meighan and they think you're delirious. Did you see Gloria in Wages of Virtue? You missed somethin'!

Well, Doc Stair hadn't been here more than a week when he came in one day to get shaved and I recognized who he was, as he had been pointed out to me, so I told him about my old lady. She's been ailin' for a couple years and either Doc Gamble or Doc Foote, neither one, seemed to be helpin' her. So he said he would come out and see her, but if she was able to get out herself, it would be better to bring her to his office where he could make a completer examination.

So I took her to his office and w'ile I was waitin' for her in the reception room, in come Julie Gregg. When somebody comes in Doc Stair's office, they's a bell that rings in his inside office so he can tell they's somebody to see him.

So he left my old lady inside and come out to the front office and that's the first time him and Julie met and I guess it was what they call love at first sight. But it wasn't fifty-fifty. This young fella was the slickest lookin' fella she'd ever seen in this town and she went wild over him. To him she was just a young lady that wanted to see the doctor.

She'd came on about the same business I had. Her mother had been doctorin' for years with Doc Gamble and Doc Foote and with" out no results. So she'd heard they was a new doc in town and decided to give him a try. He promised to call and see her mother that same day.

I said a minute ago that it was love at first sight on her part. I'm not only judgin' by how she acted afterwards but how she looked at him that first day in his office. I ain't no mind reader, but it was wrote all over her face that she was gone.

Now Jim Kendall, besides bein' a jokesmith and a pretty good drinker, well Jim was quite a lady-killer. I guess he run pretty wild durin' the time he was on the road for them Carterville people, and besides that, he'd had a couple little affairs of the heart right here in town. As I say, his wife would have divorced him, only she couldn't.

But Jim was like the majority of men, and women, too, I guess. He wanted what he couldn't get. He wanted Julie Gregg and worked his head off tryin' to land her. Only he'd of said bean instead of head.

Well, Jim's habits and his jokes didn't appeal to Julie and of course he was a married man, so he didn't have no more chance than, well, than a rabbit. That's an expression of Jim's himself. When somebody didn't have no chance to get elected or somethin', Jim would always say they didn't have no more chance than a rabbit.

He didn't make no bones about how he felt. Right in here, more than once, in front of the whole crowd, he said he was stuck on Julie and anybody that could get her for him was welcome to his house and his wife and kids included. But she wouldn't have nothin' to do with him; wouldn't even speak to him on the street. He finally seen he wasn't gettin' nowheres with his usual line so he decided to try the rough stuff. He went right up to her house one evenin' and when she opened the door he forced his way in and grabbed her. But she broke loose and before he could stop her, she run in the next room and locked the door and phoned to Joe Barnes. Joe's the marshal. Jim could hear who she was phonin' to and he beat it before Joe got there.

Joe was an old friend of Julie's pa. Joe went to Jim the next day and told him what would happen if he ever done it again.

I don't know how the news of this little affair leaked out. Chances is that Joe Barnes told his wife and she told somebody else's wife and they told their husband. Anyways, it did leak out and Hod Meyers had the nerve to kid Jim about it, right here in this shop. Jim didn't deny nothin' and kind of laughed it off and said for us all to wait; that lots of people had tried to make a monkey out of him, but he always got even.

Meanw'ile everybody in town was wise to Julie's bein' wild mad over the Doc. I don't suppose she had any idea how her face changed when him and her was together; of course she couldn't of, or she'd of kept away from him. And she didn't know that we was all noticin' how many times she made excuses to go up to his office or pass it on the other side of the street and look up in his window to see if he was there. I felt sorry for her and so did most other people.

Hod Meyers kept rubbin' it into Jim about how the Doc had cut him out. Jim didn't pay no attention to the kiddie' and you could see he was plannin' one of his jokes.

One trick Jim had was the knack of changin' his voice. He could make you think he was a girl talkie' and he could mimic any man's voice. To show you how good he was along this line, I'll tell you the joke he played on me once.

You know, in most towns of any size, when a man is dead and needs a shave, why the barber that shaves him soaks him five dollars for the job; that is, he don't soak him, but whoever ordered the shave. I just charge three dollars because personally I don't mind much shavin' a dead person. They lay a whole lot stiller than live customers. The only thing is that you don't feel like talkie' to them and you get kind of lonesome.

Well, about the coldest day we ever had here, two years ago last winter, the phone rung at the house w'ile I was home to dinner and I answered the phone and it was a woman's voice and she said she was Mrs. John Scott and her husband was dead and would I come out and shave him.

Old John had always been a good customer of mine. But they live seven miles out in the country, on the Streeter road. Still I didn't see how I could say no.

So I said I would be there, but would have to come in a jitney and it might cost three or four dollars besides the price of the shave. So she, or the voice, it said that was all right, so I got Frank Abbott to drive me out to the place and when I got there, who should open the door but old John himself! He wasn't no more dead than, well, than a rabbit.

It didn't take no private detective to figure out who had played me this little joke. Nobody could of thought it up but Jim Kendall. He certainly was a card!

I tell you this incident just to show you how he could disguise his voice and make you believe it was somebody else talkie'. I'd of swore it was Mrs. Scott had called me. Anyways, some woman.

Well, Jim waited till he had Doc Stair's voice down pat; then he went after revenge.

He called Julie up on a night when he knew Doc was over in Carterville. She never questioned but what it was Doc's voice. Jim said he must see her that night; he couldn't wait no longer to tell her somethin'. She was all excited and told him to come to the house.

But he said he was expectin' an important long distance call and wouldn't she please forget her manners for once and come to his office. He said they couldn't nothin' hurt her and nobody would see her and he just must talk to her a little w'ile. Well, poor Julie fell for it.

Doc always keeps a night light in his office, so it looked to Julie like they was somebody there.

Meanw'ile Jim Kendall had went to Wright's poolroom, where they was a whole gang amusin' themselves. The most of them had drank plenty of gin, and they was a rough bunch even when sober. They was always strong for Jim's jokes and when he told them to come with him and see some fun they give up their card games and pool games and followed along.

Doc's office is on the second floor. Right outside his door they's a flight of stairs leadin' to the floor above. Jim and his gang hid in the dark behind these stairs.

Well, tulle come up to Doc's door and rung the bell and they was nothin' coin'. She rung it again and she rung it seven or eight times. Then she tried the door and found it locked. Then Jim made some kind of a noise and she heard it and waited a minute, and then she says, "Is that you, Ralph?" Ralph is Doc's first name.

They was no answer and it must of came to her all of a sudden that she'd been bunked. She pretty near fell downstairs and the whole gang after her. They chased her all the way home, hollerin', "Is that you, Ralph?" and

"Oh, Ralphie, dear, is that you?" Jim says he couldn't holler it himself, as he was laughin' too hard.

Poor Julie! She didn't show up here on Main Street for a long, long time afterward.

And of course Jim and his gang told everybody in town, everybody but Doc Stair. They was scared to tell him, and he might of never knowed only for Paul Dickson. The poor cuckoo, as Jim called him, he was here in the shop one night when Jim was still gloatin' yet over what he'd done to Julie. And Paul took in as much of it as he could understand and he run to Doc with the story.

It's a cinch Doc went up in the air and swore he'd make Jim suffer. But it was a kind of a delicate thing, because if it got out that he had beat Jim up, Julie was bound to hear of it and then she'd know that Doc knew and of course knowin' that he knew would make it worse for her than ever. He was goin' to do somethin', but it took a lot of figurin'.

Well, it was a couple days later when Jim was here in the shop again, and so was the cuckoo. Jim was goin' duck-shootin' the next day and had come in lookin' for Hod Meyers to go with him. I happened to know that Hod had went over to Carterville and wouldn't be home till the end of the week. So Jim said he hated to go alone and he guessed he would call it off. Then poor Paul spoke up and said if Jim would take him he would go along. Jim thought a w'ile and then he said, well, he guessed a half-wit was better than nothin'.

I suppose he was plottin' to get Paul out in the boat and play some joke on him, like pushin' him in the water. Anyways, he said Paul could go. He asked him had he ever shot a duck and Paul said no, he'd never even had a gun in his hands. So Jim said he could set in the boat and watch him and if he behaved himself, he might lend him his gun for a couple of shots. They made a date to meet in the mornin' and that's the last I seen of Jim alive.

Next mornin', I hadn't been open more than ten minutes when Doc Stair come in. He looked kind of nervous. He asked me had I seen Paul Dickson. I said no, but I knew where he was, out duckshootin' with Jim Kendall. So Doc says that's what he had heard, and he couldn't understand it because Paul had told him he wouldn't never have no more to do with Jim as long as he lived.

He said Paul had told him about the joke Jim had played on Julie. He said Paul had asked him what he thought of the joke and the Doc told him that anybody that would do a thing like that ought not to be let live. I said it had been a kind of a raw thing, but Jim just couldn't resist no kind of a joke, no matter how raw. I said I thought he was all right at heart, but just bubblin' over with mischief. Doc turned and walked out.

At noon he got a phone call from old John Scott. The lake where Jim and Paul had went shootin' is on John's place. Paul had came runnin' up to the house a few minutes before and said they'd been an accident. Jim had shot a few ducks and then give the gun to Paul and told him to try his luck. Paul hadn't never handled a gun and he was nervous. He was shakin' so hard that he couldn't control the gun. He let fire and Jim sunk back in the boat, dead.

Doc Stair, bein' the coroner, jumped in Frank Abbott's flivver and rushed out to Scott's farm. Paul and old John was down on the shore of the lake. Paul had rowed the boat to shore, but they'd left the body in it, waiting for Doc to come.

Doc examined the body and said they might as well fetch it back to town. They was no use leavin' it there or callin' a jury, as it was a plain case of accidental shootin'.

Personally I wouldn't never leave a person shoot a gun in the same boat I was in unless I was sure they knew somethin' about guns. Jim was a sucker to leave a new beginner have his gun, let alone a half-wit. It probably served Jim right, what he got. But still we miss him round here. He certainly was a card! Comb it wet or dry?

The Golden Honey Moon

Mother says that when I start talking I never know when to stop. But I tell her the only time I get a chance is when she ain't around, so I have to make the most of it. I guess the fact is neither one of us would be welcome in a Quaker meeting, but as I tell Mother, what did God give us tongues for if He didn't want we should use them? Only she says He didn't give them to us to say the same thing over and over again, like I do, and repeat myself. But I say:

"Well, Mother," I say, "when people is like you and I and been married fifty years, do you expect everything I say will be something you ain't heard me say before? But it may be new to others, as they ain't nobody else lived with me as long as you have."

So she says:

"You can bet they ain't, as they couldn't nobody else stand you that long."

"Well," I tell her, "you look pretty healthy."

"Maybe I do," she will say, "but I looked even healthier before I married you."

You can't get ahead of Mother.

Yes, sir, we was married just fifty years ago the seventeenth day of last December and my daughter and son-in-law was over from Trenton to help us celebrate the Golden Wedding. My son-in-law is John H. Kramer, the real estate man. He made $12,000 one year and is pretty well thought of around Trenton; a good, steady, hard worker. The Rotarians was after him a long time to join, but he kept telling them his home was his club. But Edie finally made him join. That's my daughter.

Well, anyway, they come over to help us celebrate the Golden Wedding and it was pretty crimpy weather and the furnace don't seem to heat up no more like it used to and Mother made the remark that she hoped this winter wouldn't be as cold as the last, referring to the winter previous. So Edie said if she was us, and nothing to keep us home, she certainly wouldn't spend no more winters up here and why didn't we just shut off the water and close up the house and go down to Tampa, Florida? You know we was there four winters ago and staid five weeks, but it cost us over three hundred and fifty dollars for hotel bill alone. So Mother said we wasn't going no place to be robbed. So my son-in-law spoke up and said that Tampa wasn't the only place in the South, and besides we didn't have to stop at no high price hotel but could rent us a couple rooms and board out somewheres, and he had heard that St. Petersburg, Florida, was the spot and if we said the word he would write down there and make inquiries.

Well, to make a long story short, we decided to do it and Edie said it would be our Golden Honeymoon and for a present my son-in-law paid the difference between a section and a compartment so as we could have a compartment and have more privatecy. In a compartment you have an upper and lower berth just like the regular sleeper, but it is a shut in room by itself and got a wash bowl. The car we went in was all compartments and no regular berths at all. It was all compartments.

We went to Trenton the night before and staid at my daughter and son-in-law and we left Trenton the next afternoon at 3.23 P.M.

This was the twelfth day of January. Mother set facing the front of the train, as it makes her giddy to ride backwards. I set facing her, which does not affect me. We reached North Philadelphia at 4.03 P.M. and we reached West Philadelphia at 4.14, but did not go into Broad Street. We reached Baltimore at 6.30 and Washington, D.C., at 7.25. Our train laid over in Washington two hours till another train come along to pick us up and I got out and strolled up the platform and into the Union Station. When I come back, our car had been switched on to another track, but I remembered the name of it, the La Belle, as I had once visited my aunt out in Oconomowoc, Wisconsin, where there was a lake of that name, so I had no difficulty in getting located. But Mother had nearly fretted herself sick for fear I would be left.

"Well," I said, "I would of followed you on the next train."

"You could of," said Mother, and she pointed out that she had the money.

"Well," I said, "we are in Washington and I could of borrowed from the United States Treasury. I would of pretended I was an Englishman."

Mother caught the point and laughed heartily.

Our train pulled out of Washington at 9.40 P.M. and Mother and I turned in early, I taking the upper. During the night we passed through the green fields of old Virginia, though it was too dark to tell if they was green or what color. When we got up in the morning, we was at Fayetteville, North Carolina. We had breakfast in the dining car and after breakfast I got in conversation with the man in the next compartment to ours. He was from Lebanon, New Hampshire, and a man about eighty years of age. His wife was with him, and two unmarried daughters and I made the remark that I should think the four of them would be crowded in one compartment, but he said they had made the trip every winter for fifteen years and knowed how to keep out of each other's way. He said they was bound for Tarpon Springs.

We reached Charleston, South Carolina, at 12.50 P.M. and arrived at Savannah, Georgia, at 4.20. We reached Jacksonville, Florida, at 8.45 P.M. and had an hour and a quarter to lay over there, but Mother made a fuss about me getting off the train, so we had the darky make up our berths and retired before we left Jacksonville. I didn't sleep good as the train done a lot of hemming and hawing, and Mother never sleeps good on a train as she says she is always worrying that I will fall out. She says she would rather have the upper herself, as then she would not have to worry about me, but I tell her I can't take the risk of having it get out that I allowed my wife to sleep in an upper berth. It would make talk.

We was up in the morning in time to see our friends from New Hampshire get off at Tarpon Springs, which we reached at 6.53 A.M.

Several of our fellow passengers got off at Clearwater and some at Belleair, where the train backs right up to the door of the mammoth hotel. Belleair is the winter headquarters for the golf dudes and everybody that got off there had their bag of sticks, as many as ten and twelve in a bag. Women and all. When I was a young man we called it shinny and only needed one club to play with and about one game of it would of been a-plenty for some of these dudes, the way we played it.

The train pulled into St. Petersburg at 8.20 and when we got off the train you would think they was a riot, what with all the darkies barking for the different hotels.

I said to Mother, I said:

"It is a good thing we have got a place picked out to go to and don't have to choose a hotel, as it would be hard to choose amongst them if every one of them is the best."

She laughed.

We found a jitney and I give him the address of the room my son-in-law had got for us and soon we was there and introduced ourselves to the lady that owns the house, a young widow about forty-eight years of age. She showed us our room, which was light and airy with a comfortable bed and bureau and washstand. It was twelve dollars a week, but the location was good, only three blocks from Williams Park.

St. Pete is what folks calls the town, though they also call it the Sunshine City, as they claim they's no other place in the country where they's fewer days when Old Sol don't smile down on Mother Earth, and one of the newspapers gives away all their copies free every day when the sun don't shine. They claim to of only give them away some sixty-odd times in the last eleven years. Another nickname they have got for the town is "the Poor Man's Palm Beach," but I guess they's men that comes there that could borrow as much from the bank as some of the Willie boys over to the other Palm Beach.

During our stay we paid a visit to the Lewis Tent City, which is the headquarters for the Tin Can Tourists. But maybe you ain't heard about them. Well, they are an organization that takes their vacation trips by auto and carries everything with them. That is, they bring along their tents to sleep in and cook in and they don't patronize no hotels or cafeterias, but they have got to be bona fide auto campers or they can't belong to the organization.

They tell me they's over 200,000 members to it and they call themselves the Tin Canners on account of most of their food being put up in tin cans. One couple we seen in the Tent City was a couple from Brady, Texas, named Mr. and Mrs. Pence, which the old man is over eighty years of age and they had come in their auto all the way from home, a distance of 1,641 miles. They took five weeks for the trip, Mr. Pence driving the entire distance.

The Tin Canners hails from every State in the Union and in the summer time they visit places like New England and the Great Lakes region, but in the winter the most of them comes to Florida and scatters all over the State. While we was down there, they was a national convention of them at Gainesville, Florida, and they elected a Fredonia, New York, man as their president. His title is Royal Tin Can Opener of the

World. They have got a song wrote up which everybody has got to learn it before they are a member:

"The tin can forever! Hurrah, boys! Hurrah!

Up with the tin can! Down with the foe!

We will rally round the campfire, we'll rally once again,

Shouting, 'We auto camp forever!'"

That is something like it. And the members has also got to have a tin can fastened on to the front of their machine.

I asked Mother how she would like to travel around that way and she said:

"Fine, but not with an old rattle brain like you driving."

"Well," I said, "I am eight years younger than this Mr. Pence who drove here from Texas."

"Yes," she said, "but he is old enough to not be skittish."

You can't get ahead of Mother.

Well, one of the first things we done in St. Petersburg was to go to the Chamber of Commerce and register our names and where we was from as they's great rivalry amongst the different States in regards to the number of their citizens visiting in town and of course our little State don't stand much of a show, but still every little bit helps, as the fella says. All and all, the man told us, they was eleven thousand names registered, Ohio leading with some fifteen hundred-odd and New York State next with twelve hundred. Then come Michigan, Pennsylvania and so on down, with one man each from Cuba and Nevada.

The first night we was there, they was a meeting of the New York-New Jersey Society at the Congregational Church and a man from Ogdensburg, New York State, made the talk. His subject was Rainbow Chasing. He is a Rotarian and a very convicting speaker, though I forget his name.

Our first business, of course, was to find a place to eat and after trying several places we run on to a cafeteria on Central Avenue that suited us up and down. We eat pretty near all our meals there and it averaged about two dollars per day for the two of us, but the food was well cooked and everything nice and clean. A man don't mind paying the price if things is clean and well cooked.

On the third day of February, which is Mother's birthday, we spread ourselves and eat supper at the Poinsettia Hotel and they charged us seventy-five cents for a sirloin steak that wasn't hardly big enough for one.

I said to Mother: "Well," I said, "I guess it's a good thing every day ain't your birthday or we would be in the poorhouse."

"No," says Mother, "because if every day was my birthday, I would be old enough by this time to of been in my grave long ago."

You can't get ahead of Mother.

In the hotel they had a card-room where they was several men and ladies playing five hundred and this new fangled whist bridge. We also seen a place where they was dancing, so I asked Mother would she like to trip tne light fantastic toe and she said no, she was too old to squirm like you have got to do now days. We watched some of the young folks at it awhile till Mother got disgusted and said we would have to see a good movie to take the taste out of our mouth. Mother is a great movie heroyne and we go twice a week here at home.

But I want to tell you about the Park. The second day we was there we visited the Park, which is a good deal like the one in Tampa, only bigger, and they's more fun goes on here every day than you could shake a stick at. In the middle they's a big bandstand and chairs for the folks to set and listen to the concerts, which they give you music for all tastes, from Dixie up to classical pieces like Hearts and Flowers.

Then all around they's places marked off for different sports and games–chess and checkers and dominoes for folks that enjoys those kind of games, and roque and horse-shoes for the nimbler ones. I used to pitch a pretty fair shoe myself, but ain't done much of it in the last twenty years.

Well, anyway, we bought a membership ticket in the club which costs one dollar for the season, and they tell me that up to a couple years ago it was fifty cents, but they had to raise it to keep out the riffraff.

Well, Mother and I put in a great day watching the pitchers and she wanted I should get in the game, but I told her I was all out of practice and would make a fool of myself, though I seen several men pitching who I guess I could take their measure without no practice. However, they was some good pitchers, too, and one boy from Akron, Ohio, who could certainly throw a pretty shoe. They told me it looked like he would win them championship of the United States in the February tournament. We come away a few days before they held that and I never did hear if he win. I forget his name, but he was a clean cut young fella and he has got a brother in Cleveland that's a Rotarian.

Well, we just stood around and watched the different games for two or three days and finally I set down in a checker game with a man named Weaver from Danville, Illinois. He was a pretty fair checker player, but he wasn't no match for me, and I hope that don't sound like bragging. But I always could hold my own on a checker-board and the folks around here will tell you the same thing. I played with this Weaver pretty near all morning for two or three mornings and he beat me one game and the only other time it looked like he had a chance, the noon whistle blowed and we had to quit and go to dinner.

While I was playing checkers, Mother would set and listen to the band, as she loves music, classical or no matter what kind, but anyway she was setting there one day and between selections the woman next to her opened up a conversation. She was a woman about Mother's own age, seventy or seventy-one, and finally she asked Mother's name and Mother told her her name and where she was from and Mother asked her the same question, and who do you think the woman was?

Well, sir, it was the wife of Frank M. Hartsell, the man who was engaged to Mother till I stepped in and cut him out, fifty-two years ago!

Yes, sir!

You can imagine Mother's surprise! And Mrs. Hartsell was surprised, too, when Mother told her she had once been friends with her husband, though Mother didn't say how close friends they had been, or that Mother and I was the cause of Hartsell going out West. But that's what we was. Hartsell left his town a month after the engagement was broke off and ain't never been back since. He had went out to Michigan and become a veterinary, and that is where he had settled down, in Hillsdale, Michigan, and finally married his wife.

Well, Mother screwed up her courage to ask if Frank was still living and Mrs. Hartsell took her over to where they was pitching horse-shoes and there was old Frank, waiting his turn. And he knowed Mother as soon as he seen her, though it was over fifty years. He said he knowed her by her eyes.

"Why, it's Lucy Frost!" he says, and he throwed down his shoes and quit the game.

Then they come over and hunted me up and I will confess I wouldn't of knowed him. Him and I is the same age to the month, but he seems to show it more, some way. He is balder for one thing. And his beard is all white, where mine has still got a streak of brown in it. The very first thing I said to him, I said:

"Well, Frank, that beard of yours makes me feel like I was back north. It looks like a regular blizzard."

"Well," he said, "I guess yourn would be just as white if you had it dry cleaned."

But Mother wouldn't stand that.

"Is that so!" she said to Frank. "Well, Chancy ain't had no tobacco in his mouth for over ten years!"

And I ain't!

Well, I excused myself from the checker game and it was pretty close to noon, so we decided to all have dinner together and they was nothing for it only we must try their cafeteria on Third Avenue. It was a little more expensive than ours and not near as good, I thought. I and Mother had about the same dinner we had been having every day and our bill was $1.10. Frank's check was $1.20 for he and his wife. The same meal wouldn't of cost them more than a dollar at our place.

After dinner we made them come up to our house and we all set in the parlor, which the young woman had give us the use of to entertain company. We begun talking over old times and Mother said she was a-scared Mrs. Hartsell would find it tiresome listening to we three talk over old times, but as it turned out they wasn't much chance for nobody else to talk with Mrs. Hartsell in the company. I have heard lots of women that could go it, but Hartsell's wife takes the cake of all the women I ever seen. She told us the family history of everybody in the State of Michigan and bragged for a half hour about her son, who she said is in the drug business in Grand Rapids, and a Rotarian.

When I and Hartsell could get a word in edgeways we joked one another back and forth and I chafed him about being a horse doctor.

"Well, Frank," I said, "you look pretty prosperous, so I suppose they's been plenty of glanders around Hillsdale."

"Well," he said, "I've managed to make more than a fair living. But I've worked pretty hard."

"Yes," I said, "and I suppose you get called out all hours of the night to attend births and so on."

Mother made me shut up.

Well, I thought they wouldn't never go home and I and Mother was in misery trying to keep awake, as the both of us generally always takes a nap after dinner. Finally they went, after we had made an engagement to meet them in the Park the next morning, and Mrs. Hartsell also invited us to come to their place the next night and play five hundred. But she had forgot that they was a meeting of the Michigan Society that evening, so it was not till two evenings later that we had our first card game.

Hartsell and his wife lived in a house on Third Avenue North and had a private setting room besides their bedroom. Mrs. Hartsell couldn't quit talking about their private setting room like it was something wonderful. We played cards with them, with Mother and Hartsell partners against his wife and I. Mrs. Hartsell is a miserable card player and we certainly got the worst of it.

After the game she brought out a dish of oranges and we had to pretend it was just what we wanted, though oranges down there is like a young man's whiskers; you enjoy them at first, but they get to be a pesky nuisance.

We played cards again the next night at our place with the same partners and I and Mrs. Hartsell was beat again. Mother and Hartsell was full of compliments for each other on what a good team they made, but the both of them knowed well enough where the secret of their success laid. I guess all and all we must of played ten different evenings and they was only one night when Mrs. Hartsell and I come out ahead. And that one night wasn't no fault of hern.

When we had been down there about two weeks, we spent one evening as their guest in the Congregational Church, at a social give by the Michigan Society. A talk was made by a man named Bitting of Detroit, Michigan, on How I was Cured of Story Telling. He is a big man in the Rotarians and give a witty talk.

A woman named Mrs. Oxford rendered some selections which Mrs. Hartsell said was grand opera music, but whatever they was my daughter Edie could of give her cards and spades and not made such a hullaballoo about it neither.

Then they was a ventriloquist from Grand Rapids and a young woman about forty-five years of age that mimicked different kinds of birds. I whispered to Mother that they all sounded like a chicken, but she nudged me to shut up.

After the show we stopped in a drug store and I set up the refreshments and it was pretty close to ten o'clock before we finally turned in. Mother and I would of preferred tending the movies, but Mother said we mustn't offend Mrs. Hartsell, though I asked her had we came to Florida to enjoy ourselves or to just not offend an old chatter-box from Michigan.

I felt sorry for Hartsell one morning. The women folks both had an engagement down to the chiropodist's and I run across Hartsell in the Park and he foolishly offered to play me checkers.

It was him that suggested it, not me, and I guess he repented himself before we had played one game. But he was too stubborn to give up and set there while I beat him game after game and the worst part of it was that a crowd of folks had got in the habit of watching me play and there they all was, hooking on, and finally they seen what a fool Frank was making of himself, and they began to chafe him and pass remarks. Like one of them said:

"Who ever told you you was a checker player!"

And:

"You might maybe be good for tiddle-de-winks, but not checkers!

I almost felt like letting him beat me a couple games. But the crowd would of knowed it was a put up job.

Well, the women folks joined us in the Park and I wasn't going to mention our little game, but Hartsell told about it himself and admitted he wasn't no match for me.

"Well," said Mrs. Hartsell, "checkers ain't much of a game anyway, is it?" She said: "It's more of a children's game, ain't it? At least, I know my boy's children used to play it a good deal."

"Yes, ma'am," I said. "It's a children's game the way your husband plays it, too."

Mother wanted to smooth things over, so she said:

"Maybe they's other games where Frank can beat you."

"Yes," said Mrs. Hartsell, "and I bet he could beat you pitching horse-shoes."

"Well," I said, "I would give him a chance to try, only I ain't pitched a shoe in over sixteen years."

"Well," said Hartsell, "I ain't played checkers in twenty years."

"You ain't never played it," I said.

"Anyway," says Frank, "Lucy and I is your master at five hundred."

Well, I could of told him why that was, but had decency enough to hold my tongue.

It had got so now that he wanted to play cards every night and when I or Mother wanted to go to a movie, any one of us would have to pretend we had a headache and then trust to goodness that they wouldn't see us sneak into the theater. I don't mind playing cards when my partner keeps their mind on the game, but you take a woman like Hartsell's wife and how can they play cards when they have got to stop every couple seconds and brag about their son in Grand Rapids?

Well, the New York-New Jersey Society announced that they was goin' to give a social evening too and I said to Mother, I said:

"Well, that is one evening when we will have an excuse not to play five hundred."

"Yes," she said, "but we will have to ask Frank and his wife to go to the social with us as they asked us to go to the Michigan social."

"Well," I said, "I had rather stay home than drag that chatterbox everywheres we go."

So Mother said:

"You are getting too cranky. Maybe she does talk a little too much but she is good hearted. And Frank is always good company."

So I said:

"I suppose if he is such good company you wished you had of married him."

Mother laughed and said I sounded like I was jealous. Jealous of a cow doctor!

Anyway we had to drag them along to the social and I will say that we give them a much better entertainment than they had given us.

Judge Lane of Paterson made a fine talk on business conditions and a Mrs. Newell of Westfield imitated birds, only you could really tell what they was the way she done it. Two young women from Red Bank sung a choral selection and we clapped them back and they gave us Home to Our Mountains and Mother and Mrs. Hartsell both had tears in their eyes. And Hartsell, too.

Well, some way or another the chairman got wind that I was there and asked me to make a talk and I wasn't even going to get up, but Mother made me, so I got up and said:

"Ladies and gentlemen," I said. "I didn't expect to be called on for a speech on an occasion like this or no other occasion as I do not set myself up as a speech maker, so will have to do the best I can, which I often say is the best anybody can do."

Then I told them the story about Pat and the motorcycle, using the brogue, and it seemed to tickle them and I told them one or two other stories, hut altogether I wasn't on my feet more than twenty or twenty-five minutes and you ought to of heard the clapping and hollering when I set down. Even Mrs. Hartsell admitted that I am quite a speechifier and said if I ever went to Grand Rapids, Michigan, her son would make me talk to the Rotarians.

When it was over, Hartsell wanted we should go to their house and play cards, but his wife reminded him that it was after 9.30 P.M., rather a late hour to start a card game, but he had went crazy on the subject of cards, probably because he didn't have to play partners with his wife. Anyway, we got rid of them and went home to bed.

It was the next morning, when we met over to the Park, that Mrs. Hartsell made the remark that she wasn't getting no exercise so I suggested that why didn't she take part in the roque game.

She said she had not played a game of roque in twenty years, but if Mother would play she would play. Well, at first Mother wouldn't hear of it, but finally consented, more to please Mrs. Hartsell than anything else.

Well, they had a game with a Mrs. Ryan from Eagle, Nebraska, and a young Mrs. Morse from Rutland, Vermont, who Mother had met down to the chiropodist's. Well, Mother couldn't hit a flea and they all laughed at her and I couldn't help from laughing at her myself and finally she quit and said her back was too lame to stoop over. So they got another lady and kept on playing and soon Mrs. Hartsell was the one everybody was laughing at, as she had a long shot to hit the black ball, and as she made the effort her teeth fell out on to the court. I never seen a woman so flustered in my life. And I never heard so much laughing, only Mrs. Hartsell didn't join in and she was madder than a hornet and wouldn't play no more, so the game broke up.

Mrs. Hartsell went home without speaking to nobody, but Hartsell stayed around and finally he said to me, he said:

"Well, I played you checkers the other day and you beat me bad and now what do you say if you and me play a game of horseshoes?"

I told him I hadn't pitched a shoe in sixteen years, but Mother said:

"Go ahead and play. You used to be good at it and maybe it will come back to you."

Well, to make a long story short, I give in. I oughtn't to of never tried it, as I hadn't pitched a shoe in sixteen years, and I only done it to humor Hartsell.

Before we started, Mother patted me on the back and told me to do my best, so we started in and I seen right off that I was in for it, as I hadn't pitched a shoe in sixteen years and didn't have my distance. And besides, the plating had wore off the shoes so that they was points right where they stuck into my thumb and I hadn't throwed more than two or three times when my thumb was raw and it pretty near killed me to hang on to the shoe, let alone pitch it.

Well, Hartsell throws the awkwardest shoe I ever seen pitched and to see him pitch you wouldn't think he would ever come nowheres near, but he is also the luckiest pitcher I ever seen and he made some pitches where the shoe lit five and six feet short and then schoonered up and was a ringer. They's no use trying to beat that kind of luck.

They was a pretty fair size crowd watching us and four or five other ladies besides Mother, and it seems like, when Hartsell pitches, he has got to chew and it kept the ladies on the anxious seat as he don't seem to care which way he is facing when he leaves go.

You would think a man as old as him would of learnt more manners.

Well, to make a long story short, I was just beginning to get my distance when I had to give up on account of my thumb, which I showed it to Hartsell and he seen I couldn't go on, as it was raw and bleeding. Even if I could of stood it to go on myself, Mother wouldn't of allowed it after she seen my thumb. So anyway I quit and Hartsell said the score was nineteen to six, but I don't know what it was. Or don't care, neither.

Well, Mother and I went home and I said I hoped we was through with the Hartsells as I was sick and tired of them, but it seemed like she had promised we would go over to their house that evening for another game of their everlasting cards.

Well, my thumb was giving me considerable pain and I felt kind of out of sorts and I guess maybe I forgot myself, but anyway, when we was about through playing Hartsell made the remark that he wouldn't never lose a game of cards if he could always have Mother for a partner.

So I said:

"Well, you had a chance fifty years ago to always have her for a partner, but you wasn't man enough to keep her."

I was sorry the minute I had said it and Hartsell didn't know what to say and for once his wife couldn't say nothing. Mother tried to smooth things over by making the remark that I must of had something stronger than tea or I wouldn't talk so silly. But Mrs. Hartsell had froze up like an iceberg and hardly said good night to us and I bet her and Frank put in a pleasant hour after we was gone.

As we was leaving, Mother said to him: "Never mind Charley's nonsense, Frank. He is just mad because you beat him all hollow pitching horseshoes and playing cards."

She said that to make up for my slip, but at the same time she certainly riled me. I tried to keep ahold of myself, but as soon as we was out of the house she had to open up the subject and begun to scold me for the break I had made.

Well, I wasn't in no mood to be scolded. So I said: "I guess he is such a wonderful pitcher and card player that you wished you had married him."

"Well," she said, "at least he ain't a baby to give up pitching because his thumb has got a few scratches."

"And how about you," I said, "making a fool of yourself on the roque court and then pretemiding your back is lame and you can't play no more!"

"Yes," she said, "but when you hurt your thumb I didn't laugh at you, and why did you laugh at me when I sprained my back?"

"Who could help from laughing!" I said.

"Well," she said, "Frank Hartsell didn't laugh."

"Well," I said, "why didn't you marry him?"

"Well," said Mother, "I almost wished I had!"

"And I wished so, too!" I said.

"I'll remember that!" said Mother, and that's the last word she said to me for two days.

We seen the Hartsells the next day in the Park and I was willing to apologize, but they just nodded to us. And a couple days later we heard they had left for Orlando, where they have got relatives.

I wished they had went there in the first place.

Mother and I made it up setting on a bench.

"Listen, Charley," she said. "This is our Golden Honeymoon and we don't want the whole thing spoilt with a silly old quarrel."

"Well," I said, "did you mean that about wishing you had married Hartsell?"

"Of course not," she said, "that is, if you didn't mean that you wished I had, too." So I said:

"I was just tired and all wrought up. I thank God you chose me instead of him as they's no other woman in the world who I could of lived with all these years."

"How about Mrs. Hartsell?" says Mother.

"Good gracious!" I said. "Imagine being married to a woman that plays five hundred like she does and drops her teeth on the roque court!"

"Well," said Mother, "it wouldn't be no worse than being married to a man that expectorates towards ladies and is such a fool in a checker game."

So I put my arm around her shoulder and she stroked my hand and I guess we got kind of spoony.

They was two days left of our stay in St. Petersburg and the next to the last day Mother introduced me to a Mrs. Kendall from Kingston, Rhode Island, who she had met at the chiropodist's.

Mrs. Kendall made us acquainted with her husband, who is in the grocery business. They have got two sons and five grandchildren and one great-grandchild. One of their sons lives in Providence and is way up in the Elks as well as a Rotarian.

We found them very congenial people and we played cards with them the last two nights we was there. They was both experts and I only wished we had met them sooner instead of running into the Hartsells. But the Kendalls will be there again next winter and we will see more of them, that is, if we decide to make the trip again.

We left the Sunshine City on the eleventh day of February, at 11 A.M. This give us a day trip through Florida and we seen all the country we had passed through at night on the way down.

We reached Jacksonville at 7 P.M. and pulled out of there at 8.10 P.M. We reached Fayetteville, North Carolina, at nine o'clock the following morning, and reached Washington, D. C., at 6.30 P.M., laying over there half an hour.

We reached Trenton at 11.01 P.M. and had wired ahead to my daughter and son-in-law and they met us at the train and we went to their house and they put us up for the night. John would of made us stay up all night, telling about our trip, but Edie said we must be tired and made us go to bed. That's my daughter.

The next day we took our train for home and arrived safe and sound, having been gone just one month and a day.

Here comes Mother, so I guess I better shut up.

My Roomy

I

No—I ain't signed for next year; but there won't be no trouble about that. The dough part of it is all fixed up. John and me talked it over and I'll sign as soon as they send me a contract. All I told him was that he'd have to let me pick my own roommate after this and not sic no wild man on to me.

You know I didn't hit much the last two months o' the season. Some o' the boys, I notice, wrote some stuff about me gettin' old and losin' my battin' eye. That's all bunk! The reason I didn't hit was because I wasn't gettin' enough sleep. And the reason for that was Mr. Elliott.

He wasn't with us after the last part o' May, but I roomed with him long enough to get the insomny. I was the only guy in the club game enough to stand for him; but I was sorry afterward that I done it, because it sure did put a crimp in my little old average.

And do you know where he is now? I got a letter today and I'll read it to you. No—I guess I better tell you somethin' about him first. You fellers never got acquainted with him and you ought to hear the dope to understand the letter. I'll make it as short as I can.

He didn't play in no league last year. He was with some semi-pros over in Michigan and somebody writes John about him. So John sends Needham over to look at him. Tom stayed there Saturday and Sunday, and seen him work twice. He was playin' the outfield, but as luck would have it they wasn't a fly ball hit in his direction in both games. A base hit was made out his way and he booted it, and that's the only report Tom could get on his fieldin'. But he wallops two over the wall in one day and they catch two line drives off him. The next day he gets four blows and two o' them is triples.

So Tom comes back and tells John the guy is a whale of a hitter and fast as Cobb, but he don't know nothin' about his fieldin'. Then John signs him to a contract—twelve hundred or somethin' like that. We'd been in Tampa a week before he showed up. Then he comes to the hotel and just sits round all day, without tellin' nobody who he was. Finally the bellhops was going to chase him out and he says he's one o' the ballplayers. Then the clerk gets John to go over and talk to him. He tells John his name and says he hasn't had nothin' to eat for three days, because he was broke. John told me afterward that he'd drew about three hundred advance—last winter sometime. Well, they took him in the dinin' room and they tell me he inhaled about four meals at once. That night they roomed him with Heine.

Next mornin' Heine and me walks out to the grounds together and Heine tells me about him. He says:

"Don't never call me a bug again. They got me roomin' with the champion o' the world."

"Who is he?" I says.

"I don't know and I don't want to know," says Heine; "but if they stick him in there with me again I'll jump to the Federals. To start with, he ain't got no baggage. I ast him where his trunk was and he says he didn't have none. Then I ast him if he didn't have no suitcase, and he says: 'No. What do you care?' I was goin' to lend him some pajamas, but he put on the shirt o' the uniform John give him last night and slept in that. He was asleep when I got up this mornin'. I seen his collar layin' on the dresser and it looked like he had wore it in Pittsburgh every day for a year. So I throwed it out the window and he comes down to breakfast with no collar. I ast him what size collar he wore and he says he didn't want none, because he wasn't goin' out nowheres. After breakfast he beat it up to the room again and put on his uniform. When I got up there he was lookin' in the glass at himself, and he done it all the time I was dressin.'"

When we got out to the park I got my first look at him. Pretty good-lookin' guy, too, in his unie—big shoulders and well put together; built somethin' like Heine himself. He was talkin' to John when I come up.

"What position do you play?" John was askin' him.

"I play anywheres," says Elliott.

"You're the kind I'm lookin' for," says John. Then he says: "You was an outfielder up there in Michigan, wasn't you?"

"I don't care where I play," says Elliott.

John sends him to the outfield and forgets all about him for a while. Pretty soon Miller comes in and says:

"I ain't goin' to shag for no bush outfielder!"

John ast him what was the matter, and Miller tells him that Elliott ain't doin' nothin' but just standin' out there; that he ain't makin' no attemp' to catch the fungoes, and that he won't even chase 'em. Then John starts watchin' him, and it was just like Miller said. Larry hit one pretty near in his lap and he stepped out o' the way. John calls him in and ast him:

"Why don't you go after them fly balls?"

"Because I don't want 'em," says Elliott.

John gets sarcastic and says:

"What do you want? Of course we'll see that you get anythin' you want!"

"Give me a ticket back home," says Elliott.

"Don't you want to stick with the club?" says John, and the busher tells him, no, he certainly did not.

Then John tells him he'll have to pay his own fare home and Elliott don't get sore at all. He just says:

"Well, I'll have to stick, then—because I'm broke."

We was havin' battin' practice and John tells him to go up and hit a few. And you ought to of seen him bust 'em!

Lavender was in there workin' and he'd been pitchin' a little all winter, so he was in pretty good shape. He lobbed one up to Elliott, and he hit it 'way up in some trees outside the fence—about a mile, I guess. Then John tells Jimmy to put somethin' on the ball. Jim comes through with one of his fast ones and the kid slams it agin the right-field wall on a line.

"Give him your spitter!" yells John, and Jim handed him one. He pulled it over first base so fast that Bert, who was standin' down there, couldn't hardly duck in time. If it'd hit him it'd killed him.

Well, he kep' on hittin' everythin' Jim give him—and Jim had somethin' too. Finally John gets Pierce warmed up and sends him out to pitch, tellin' him to hand Elliott a flock o' curve balls. He wanted to see if lefthanders was goin' to bother him. But he slammed 'em right along, and I don't b'lieve he hit more'n two the whole mornin' that wouldn't of been base hits in a game.

They sent him out to the outfield again in the afternoon, and after a lot o' coaxin' Leach got him to go after fly balls; but that's all he did do—just go after 'em.

One hit him on the bean and another on the shoulder. He run back after the short ones and 'way in after the ones that went over his head. He catched just one—a line drive that he couldn't get out o' the way of; and then he acted like it hurt his hands.

I come back to the hotel with John. He ast me what I thought of Elliott.

"Well," I says, "he'd be the greatest ballplayer in the world if he could just play ball. He sure can bust 'em."

John says he was afraid he couldn't never make an outfielder out o' him. He says:

"I'll try him on the infield to-morrow. They must be Some place he can play. I never seen a lefthand hitter that looked so good agin lefthand pitchin'—and he's got a great arm; but he acts like he'd never saw a fly ball."

Well, he was just as bad on the infield. They put him at short and he was like a sieve. You could of drove a hearse between him and second base without him gettin' near it. He'd stoop over for a ground ball about the time it was bouncin' up agin the fence; and when he'd try to cover the bag on a peg he'd trip over it.

They tried him at first base and sometimes he'd run 'way over in the coachers' box and sometimes out in right field lookin' for the bag. Once Heine shot one acrost at him on a line and he never touched it with his hands. It went bam! right in the pit of his stomach—and the lunch he'd ate didn't do him no good.

Finally John just give up and says he'd have to keep him on the bench and let him earn his pay by bustin' 'em a couple o' times a week or so. We all agreed with John that this bird would be a whale of a pinch hitter—and we was right too. He was hittin' 'way over five hundred when the blowoff come, along about the last o' May.

II

Before the trainin' trip was over, Elliott had roomed with pretty near everybody in the club. Heine raised an awful holler after the second night down there and John put the bug in with Needham. Tom stood him for three nights. Then he doubled up with Archer, and Schulte, and Miller, and Leach, and Saier—and the whole bunch in turn, averagin' about two nights with each one before they put up a kick. Then John tried him with some o' the youngsters, but they wouldn't stand for him no more'n the others. They all said he was crazy and they was afraid he'd get violent some night and stick a knife in 'em.

He always insisted on havin' the water run in the bathtub all night, because he said it reminded him of the sound of the dam near his home. The fellers might get up four or five times a night and shut off the faucet, but he'd get right up after 'em and turn it on again. Carter, a big bush pitcher from Georgia, started a fight with him about it one night, and Elliott pretty near killed him. So the rest o' the bunch, when they'd saw Carter's map next mornin', didn't have the nerve to do nothin' when it come their turn.

Another o' his habits was the thing that scared 'em, though. He'd brought a razor with him—in his pocket, I guess—and he used to do his shavin' in the middle o' the night. Instead o' doin' it in the bathroom he'd lather his face and then come out and stand in front o' the lookin'-glass on the dresser. Of course he'd have all the lights turned on, and that was bad enough when a feller wanted to sleep; but the worst of it was that he'd stop shavin' every little while and turn round and stare at the guy who was makin' a failure o' tryin' to sleep. Then he'd wave his razor round in the air and laugh, and begin shavin' agin. You can imagine how comf'table his roomies felt!

John had bought him a suitcase and some clothes and things, and charged 'em up to him. He'd drew so much dough in advance that he didn't have nothin' comin' till about June. He never thanked John and he'd wear one shirt and one collar till some one throwed 'em away.

Well, we finally gets to Indianapolis, and we was goin' from there to Cincy to open. The last day in Indianapolis John come and ast me how I'd like to change roomies. I says I was perfectly satisfied with Larry. Then John says:

"I wisht you'd try Elliott. The other boys all kicks on him, but he seems to hang round you a lot and I b'lieve you could get along all right."

"Why don't you room him alone?" I ast.

"The boss or the hotels won't stand far us roomin' alone," says John. "You go ahead and try it, and see how you make out. If he's too much for you let me know; but he likes you and I think he'll be diff'rent with a guy who can talk to him like you can."

So I says I'd tackle it, because I didn't want to throw John down. When we got to Cincy they stuck Elliott and me in one room, and we was together till he quit us.

III

I went to the room early that night, because we was goin' to open next day and I wanted to feel like somethin'. First thing I done when I got undressed was turn on both faucets in the bathtub. They was makin' an awful racket when Elliott finally come in about midnight. I was layin' awake and I opened right up on him. I says:

"Don't shut off that water, because I like to hear it run."

Then I turned over and pretended to be asleep. The bug got his clothes off, and then what did he do but go in the bathroom and shut off the water! Then he come back in the room and says: "I guess no one's goin' to tell me what to do in here."

But I kep' right on pretendin' to sleep and didn't pay no attention. When he'd got into his bed I jumped out o' mine and turned on all the lights and begun stroppin' my razor. He says:

"What's comin' off?"

"Some o' my whiskers," I says. "I always shave along about this time."

"No, you don't!" he says. "I was in your room one mornin' down in Louisville and I seen you shavin' then."

"Well," I says, "the boys tell me you shave in the middle o' the night; and I thought if I done all the things you do mebbe I'd get so's I could hit like you."

"You must be superstitious!" he says. And I told him I was. "I'm a good hitter," he says, "and I'd be a good hitter if I never shaved at all. That don't make no diff'rence."

"Yes, it does," I says. "You prob'ly hit good because you shave at night; but you'd be a better fielder if you shaved in the mornin'."

You see, I was tryin' to be just as crazy as him—though that wasn't hardly possible.

"If that's right," says he, "I'll do my shavin' in the mornin'—because I seen in the papers where the boys says that if I could play the outfield like I can hit I'd be as good as Cobb. They tell me Cobb gets twenty thousand a year."

"No," I says; "he don't get that much—but he gets about ten times as much as you do."

"Well," he says, "I'm goin' to be as good as him, because I need the money."

"What do you want with money? " I says.

He just laughed and didn't say nothin'; but from that time on the water didn't run in the bathtub nights and he done his shavin' after breakfast. I didn't notice, though, that he looked any better in fieldin' practice.

IV

It rained one day in Cincy and they trimmed us two out o' the other three; but it wasn't Elliott's fault.

They had Larry beat four to one in the ninth innin' o' the first game. Archer gets on with two out, and John sends my roomy up to hit—though Benton, a lefthander, is workin' for them. The first thing Benton serves up there Elliott cracks it a mile over Hobby's head. It would of been good for three easy—only Archer—playin' safe, o' course—pulls up at third base. Tommy couldn't do nothin' and we was licked.

The next day he hits one out o' the park off the Indian; but we was 'way behind and they was nobody on at the time. We copped the last one without usin' no pinch hitters.

I didn't have no trouble with him nights durin' the whole series. He come to bed pretty late while we was there and I told him he'd better not let John catch him at it. "What would he do?" he says.

"Fine you fifty," I says.

"He can't fine me a dime," he says, "because I ain't got it."

Then I told him he'd be fined all he had comin' if he didn't get in the hotel before midnight; but he just laughed and says he didn't think John had a kick comin' so long as he kep' bustin' the ball.

"Some day you'll go up there and you won't bust it," I says.

"That'll be an accident," he says.

That stopped me and I didn't say nothin'. What could you say to a guy who hated himself like that?

The "accident" happened in St. Louis the first day. We needed two runs in the eighth and Saier and Brid was on, with two out. John tells Elliott to go up in Pierce's place. The bug goes up and Griner gives him two bad balls—'way outside. I thought they was goin' to walk him—and it looked like good judgment, because they'd heard what he done in Cincy. But no! Griner comes back with a fast one right over and Elliott pulls it down the right foul line, about two foot foul. He hit it so hard you'd of thought they'd sure walk him then; but Griner gives him another fast one. He slammed it again just as hard, but foul. Then Griner gives him one 'way outside and it's two and three. John says, on the bench:

"If they don't walk him now he'll bust that fence down."

I thought the same and I was sure Griner wouldn't give him nothin' to hit; but he come with a curve and Rigler calls Elliott out. From where we sat the last one looked low, and I thought Elliott'd make a kick. He come back to the bench smilin'.

John starts for his position, but stopped and ast the bug what was the matter with that one. Any busher I ever knowed would of said, "It was too low," or "It was outside," or "It was inside." Elliott says:

"Nothin' at all. It was right over the middle."

"Why didn't you bust it, then?" says John.

"I was afraid I'd kill somebody," says Elliott, and laughed like a big boob. John was pretty near chokin'.

"What are you laughin' at?" he says.

"I was thinkin' of a nickel show I seen in Cincinnati," says the bug.

"Well," says John, so mad he couldn't hardly see, "that show and that laugh'll cost you fifty."

We got beat, and I wouldn't of blamed John if he'd fined him his whole season's pay.

Up 'n the room that night I told him he'd better cut out that laughin' stuff when we was gettin' trimmed or he never would have no pay day. Then he got confidential.

"Pay day wouldn't do me no good," he says. "When I'm all squared up with the club and begin to have a pay day I'll only get a hundred bucks at a time, and I'll owe that to some o' you fellers. I wisht we could win the pennant and get in on that World's Series dough. Then I'd get a bunch at once."

"What would you do with a bunch o' dough?" I ast him.

"Don't tell nobody, sport," he says; "but if I ever get five hundred at once I'm goin' to get married."

"Oh!" I says. "And who's the lucky girl?"

"She's a girl up in Muskegon," says Elliott; "and you're right when you call her lucky."

"You don't like yourself much, do you?" I says.

"I got reason to like myself," says he. "You'd like yourself, too, if you could hit 'em like me."

"Well," I says. "you didn't show me no hittin' to-day."

"I couldn't hit because I was laughin' too hard," says Elliott.

"What was it you was laughin' at?" I says.

"I was laughin' at that pitcher," he says. "He thought he had somethin' and he didn't have nothin.'"

"He had enough to whiff you with," I says.

"He didn't have nothin'!" says he again. "I was afraid if I busted one off him they'd can him, and then I couldn't never hit agin him no more."

Naturally I didn't have no comeback to that. I just sort o' gasped and got ready to go to sleep; but he wasn't through.

"I wisht you could see this bird!" he says.

"What bird?" I says.

"This dame that's nuts about me," he says.

"Good-looker?" I ast.

"No," he says; "she ain't no bear for looks. They ain't nothin' about her for a guy to rave over till you hear her sing. She sure can holler some."

"What kind o' voice has she got?" I ast.

"A bear," says he."

"No," I says; "I mean is she a barytone or an air?"

"I don't know," he says; "but she's got the loudest voice I ever hear on a woman. She's pretty near got me beat."

"Can you sing?" I says; and I was sorry right afterward that I ast him that question.

I guess it must of been bad enough to have the water runnin' night after night and to have him wavin' that razor round; but that couldn't of been nothin' to his singin'. Just as soon as I'd pulled that boner he says, "Listen to me!" and starts in on 'Silver Threads Among the Gold.' Mind you, it was after midnight and they was guests all round us tryin' to sleep!

They used to be noise enough in our club when we had Hofman and Sheckard and Richie harmonizin'; but this bug's voice was louder'n all o' theirn combined. We once had a pitcher named Martin Walsh—brother o' Big Ed's—and I thought he could drownd out the Subway; but this guy made a boiler factory sound like Dummy Taylor. If the whole hotel wasn't awake when he'd howled the first line it's a pipe they was when he cut loose, which he done when he come to "Always young and fair to me." Them words could of been heard easy in East St. Louis.

He didn't get no encore from me, but he goes right through it again—or starts to. I knowed somethin' was goin' to happen before he finished—and somethin' did. The night clerk and the house detective come bangin' at the door. I let 'em in and they had plenty to say. If we made another sound the whole club'd be canned out o' the hotel. I tried to salve 'em, and I says:

"He won't sing no more."

But Elliott swelled up like a poisoned pup.

"Won't I?" he says. "I'll sing all I want to."

"You won't sing in here," says the clerk.

"They ain't room for my voice in here anyways," he says. "I'll go outdoors and sing."

And he puts his clothes on and ducks out. I didn't make no attemp' to stop him. I heard him bellowin' 'Silver Threads' down the corridor and dawn the stairs, with the clerk and the dick chasin' him all the way and tellin' him to shut up.

Well, the guests make a holler the next mornin'; and the hotel people tells Charlie Williams that he'll either have to let Elliott stay somewheres else or the whole club'll have to move. Charlie tells John, and John was thinkin' o' settlin' the question by releasin' Elliott.

I guess he'd about made up his mind to do it; but that afternoon they had us three to one in the ninth, and we got the bases full, with two down and Larry's turn to hit. Elliott had been sittin' on the bench sayin' nothin'.

"Do you think you can hit one today?" says John.

"I can hit one any day," says Elliott.

"Go up and hit that lefthander, then," says John, "and remember there's nothin' to laugh at."

Sallee was workin'—and workin' good; but that didn't bother the bug. He cut into one, and it went between Oakes and Whitted like a shot. He come into third standin' up and we was a run to the good. Sallee was so sore he kind o' forgot himself and took pretty near his full wind-up pitchin' to Tommy. And what did Elliott do but steal home and get away with it clean!

Well, you couldn't can him after that, could you? Charlie gets him a room somewheres and I was relieved of his company that night. The next evenin' we beat it for Chi to play about two weeks at home. He didn't tell nobody where he roomed there and I didn't see nothin' of him, 'cep' out to the park. I ast him what he did with himself nights and he says:

"Same as I do on the road—borrow some dough same place and go to the nickel shows."

"You must be stuck on 'em," I says.

"Yes." he says; "I like the ones where they kill people—because I want to learn how to do it. I may have that job some day."

"Don't pick on me," I says.

"Oh," says the bug, "you never can tell who I'll pick on."

It seemed as if he just couldn't learn nothin' about fieldin', and finally John told him to keep out o' the practice.

"A ball might hit him in the temple and croak him," says John. But he busted up a couple o' games for us at home, beatin' Pittsburgh once and Cincy once.

V

They give me a great big room at the hotel in Pittsburgh; so the fellers picked it out for the poker game. We was playin' along about ten o'clock one night when in come Elliott—the earliest he'd showed up since we'd been roomin' together. They was only five of us playin' and Tom ast him to sit in.

"I'm busted," he says.

"Can you play poker?" I ast him.

"They's nothin' I can't do!" he says. "Slip me a couple o' bucks and I'll show you."

So I slipped him a couple o' bucks and honestly hoped he'd win, because I knowed he never had no dough. Well, Tom dealt him a hand and he picks it up and says:

"I only got five cards."

"How many do you want?" I says.

"Oh," he says, "if that's all I get I'll try to make 'em do."

The pot was cracked and raised, and he stood the raise. I says to myself: "There goes my two bucks!" But no—he comes out with three queens and won the dough. It was only about seven bucks; but you'd of thought it was a million to see him grab it. He laughed like a kid.

"Guess I can't play this game!" he says; and he had me fooled for a minute—I thought he must of been kiddin' when he complained of only havin' five cards.

He copped another pot right afterward and was sittin' there with about eleven bucks in front of him when Jim opens a roodle pot for a buck. I stays and so does Elliott. Him and Jim both drawed one card and I took three. I had kings or queens—I forget which. I didn't help 'em none; so when Jim bets a buck I throws my hand away.

"How much can I bet?" says the bug.

"You can raise Jim a buck if you want to," I says.

So he bets two dollars. Jim comes back at him. He comes right back at Jim. Jim raises him again and he tilts Jim right back. Well, when he'd boosted Jim with the last buck he had, Jim says:

"I'm ready to call. I guess you got me beat. What have you got?"

"I know what I've got, all right," says Elliott. "I've got a straight." And he throws his hand down. Sure enough, it was a straight, eight high. Jim pretty near fainted and so did I.

The bug had started pullin' in the dough when Jim stops him.

"Here! Wait a minute!" says Jim. "I thought you had somethin'. I filled up." Then Jim lays down his nine full.

"You beat me, I guess," says Elliott, and he looked like he'd lost his last friend.

"Beat you?" says Jim. "Of course I beat you! What did you think I had?"

"Well," says the bug, "I thought you might have a small flush or somethin'."

When I regained consciousness he was beggin' for two more bucks.

"What for?" I says. "To play poker with? You're barred from the game for life!"

"Well," he says, "if I can't play no more I want to go to sleep, and you fellers will have to get out o' this room."

Did you ever hear o' nerve like that? This was the first night he'd came in before twelve and he orders the bunch out so's he can sleep! We politely suggested to him to go to Brooklyn.

Without sayin' a word he starts in on his 'Silver Threads' and it wasn't two minutes till the game was busted up and the bunch—all but me—was out o' there. I'd of beat it too, only be stopped yellin' as soon as they'd went.

"You're same buster!" I says. "You bust up ball games in the afternoon and poker games at night."

"Yes," he says; "that's my business—bustin' things." And before I knowed what he was about he picked up the pitcher of ice-water that was on the floor and throwed it out the window—through the glass and all.

Right then I give him a plain talkin' to. I tells him how near he come to gettin' canned down in St. Louis because he raised so much Cain singin' in the hotel.

"But I had to keep my voice in shape," he says. "If I ever get dough enough to get married the girl and me'll go out singin' together."

"Out where?" I ast.

"Out on the vaudeville circuit," says Elliott.

"Well," I says, "if her voice is like yours you'll be wastin' money if you travel round. Just stay up in Muskegon and we'll hear you, all right!"

I told him he wouldn't never get no dough if he didn't behave himself. That, even if we got in the World's Series, he wouldn't be with us—unless he cut out the foolishness.

"We ain't goin' to get in no World's Series," he says, "and I won't never get a bunch o' money at once; so it looks like I couldn't get married this fall."

Then I told him we played a city series every fall. He'd never thought o' that and it tickled him to death. I told him the losers always got about five hundred apiece and that we were about due to win it and get about eight hundred. "But," I says, " we still got a good chance for the old pennant; and if I was you I wouldn't give up hope o' that yet—not where John can hear you, anyway."

"No," he says, "we won't win no pennant, because he won't let mime play reg'lar; but I don't care so long as we're sure o' that city-series dough."

"You ain't sure of it if you don't behave," I says.

"Well," says he, very serious, "I guess I'll behave." And he did—till we made our first Eastern trip.

VI

I went to Boston first, and that crazy bunch goes out and piles up a three-run lead on us in seven innin's the first day. It was the pitcher's turn to lead off in the eighth, so up goes Elliott to bat for him. He kisses the first thing they hands him for three bases; and we says, on the bench: "Now we'll get 'em!"—because, you know, a three-run lead wasn't nothin' in Boston.

"Stay right on that bag!" John hollers to Elliott.

Mebbe if John hadn't said nothin' to him everythin' would of been all right; but when Perdue starts to pitch the first ball to Tommy, Elliott starts to steal home. He's out as far as from here to Seattle.

If I'd been carryin' a gun I'd of shot him right through the heart. As it was, I thought John'd kill him with a bat, because he was standin' there with a couple of 'em, waitin' for his turn; but I guess John was too stunned to move. He didn't even seem to see Elliott when he went to the bench. After I'd cooled off a little I says:

"Beat it and get into your clothes before John comes in. Then go to the hotel and keep out o' sight."

When I got up in the room afterward, there was Elliott, lookin' as innocent and happy as though he'd won fifty bucks with a pair o' treys.

"I thought you might of killed yourself," I says.

"What for?" he says.

"For that swell play you made," says I.

"What was the matter within the play?" ast Elliott, surprised. "It was all right when I done it in St. Louis."

"Yes," I says; "but they was two out in St. Louis and we wasn't no three runs behind."

"Well," he says, "if it was all right in St. Louis I don't see why it was wrong here."

"It's a diff'rent climate here," I says, too disgusted to argue with him.

"I wonder if they'd let me sing in this climate?" says Elliott.

"Na," I says. "Don't sing in this hotel, because we don't want to get fired out o' here—the eats is too good."

"All right," he says. "I won't sing." But when I starts down to supper he says: "I'm li'ble to do somethin' worse'n sing."

He didn't show up in the dinin' roam and John went to the boxin' show after supper; so it looked like him and Elliott wouldn't run into each other till the murder had left John's heart. I was glad o' that—because a Mass'chusetts jury might not consider it justifiable hommercide if one guy croaked another for givin' the Boston club a game.

I went down to the corner and had a couple o' beers; and then came straight back, intendin' to hit the hay. The elevator boy had went for a drink or somethin', and they was two old ladies already waitin' in the car when I stepped in. Right along after me comes Elliott.

"Where's the boy that's supposed to run this car?" he says. I told him the boy'd be right back; but he says: "I can't wait. I'm much too sleepy."

And before I could stop him he'd slammed the door and him and I and the poor old ladies was shootin' up.

"Let us off at the third floor, please!" says one o' the ladies, her voice kind o' shakin'.

"Sorry, madam," says the bug; "but this is a express and we don't stop at no third floor."

I grabbed his arm and tried to get him away from the machinery; but he was as strong as a ox and he throwed me agin the side o' the car like I was a baby. We went to the top faster'n I ever rode in an elevator before. And then we shot dawn to the bottom, hittin' the bumper down there so hard I thought we'd be smashed to splinters.

The ladies was too scared to make a sound durin' the first trip; but while we was goin' up and down the second time—even faster'n the first—they begun to scream. I was hollerin' my head off at him to quit and he was makin' more noise than the three of us—pretendin' he was the locomotive and the whole crew o' the train.

Don't never ask me how many times we went up and dawn! The women fainted on the third trip and I guess I was about as near it as I'll ever get. The elevator boy and the bellhops and the waiters and the night clerk and everybody was jumpin' round the lobby screamin'; but no one seemed to know how to stop us.

Finally—on about the tenth trip, I guess—he slowed down and stopped at the fifth floor, where we was roomin'. He opened the door and beat it for the room, while I, though I was tremblin' like a leaf, run the car down to the bottom.

The night clerk knowed me pretty well and knowed I wouldn't do nothin' like that; so him and I didn't argue, but just got to work together to bring the old women to. While we was doin' that Elliott must of run down the stairs and slipped out o' the hotel, because when they sent the officers up to the room after him he'd blowed.

They was goin' to fire the club out; but Charlie had a good stand-in with Amos, the proprietor, and he fixed it up to let us stay—providin' Elliott kep' away. The bug didn't show up at the ball park next day and we didn't see no more of him till we got on the rattler far New York. Charlie and John both bawled him, but they give him a berth—an upper—and we pulled into the Grand Central Station without him havin' made no effort to wreck the train.

VII

I'd studied the thing pretty careful, but hadn't come to no conclusion. I was sure he wasn't no stew, because none o' the boys had ever saw him even take a glass o' beer, and I couldn't never detect the odor o' booze on him. And if he'd been a dope I'd of knew about it—roomin' with him.

There wouldn't of been no mystery about it if he'd been a lefthand pitcher—but he wasn't. He wasn't nothin' but a whale of a hitter and he throwed with his right arm. He hit lefthanded, o' course; but so did Saier and Brid and Schulte and me, and John himself; and none of us was violent. I guessed he must of been just a plain nut and li'ble to break out any time.

They was a letter waitin' for him at New York, and I took it, intendin' to give it to him at the park, because I didn't think they'd let him room at the hotel; but after breakfast he come up to the room, with his suitcase. It seems he'd promised John and Charlie to be good, and made it so strong they b'lieved him.

I give him his letter, which was addressed in a girl's writin' and came from Muskegon.

"From the girl?" I says.

"Yes," he says; and, without openin' it, he tore it up and throwed it out the window.

"Had a quarrel?" I ast.

"No, no," he says; "but she can't tell me nothin' I don't know already. Girls always writes the same junk. I got one from her in Pittsburgh, but I didn't read it."

"I guess you ain't so stuck on her," I says.

He swells up and says:

"Of course I'm stuck on her! If I wasn't, do you think I'd be goin' round with this bunch and gettin' insulted all the time? I'm stickin' here because o' that series dough, so's I can get hooked."

"Do you think you'd settle down if you was married?" I ast him.

"Settle down?" he says. "Sure, I'd settle down. I'd be so happy that I wouldn't have to look for no excitement."

Nothin' special happened that might 'cep' that he come in the room about one o'clock and wake me up by pickin' up the foot o' the bed and droppin' it on the floor, sudden-like.

"Give me a key to the room," he says.

"You must of had a key," I says, "or you couldn't of got in."

"That's right!" he says, and beat it to bed.

One o' the reporters must of told Elliott that John had ast for waivers on him and New York had refused to waive, because next mornin' he come to me with that dope.

"New York's goin' to win this pennant!" he says.

"Well," I says, "they will if some one else don't. But what of it?"

"I'm goin' to play with New York," he says, "so's I can get the World's Series dough."

"How you goin' to get away from this club?" I ast.

"Just watch me!" he says. "I'll be with New York before this series is over."

Well, the way he goes after the job was original, anyway. Rube'd had one of his good days the day before and we'd got a trimmin'; but this second day the score was tied up at two runs apiece in the tenth, and Big Jeff'd been wobblin' for two or three innin's.

Well, he walks Saier and me, with one out, and Mac sends for Matty, who was warmed up and ready. John sticks Elliott in in Brid's place and the bug pulls one into the right-field stand.

It's a cinch McGraw thinks well of him then, and might of went after him if he hadn't went crazy the next afternoon. We're tied up in the ninth and Matty's workin'. John sends Elliott up with the bases choked; but he doesn't go right up to the plate. He walks over to their bench and calls McGraw out. Mac tells us about it afterward.

"I can bust up this game right here!" says Elliott.

"Go ahead," says Mac; "but be careful he don't whiff you."

Then the bug pulls it.

"If I whiff," he says, "will you get me on your club?"

"Sure!" says Mac, just as anybody would.

By this time Bill Koem was hollerin' about the delay; so up goes Elliott and gives the worst burlesque on tryin' to hit that you ever see. Matty throws one a mile outside and high, and the bug swings like it was right over the heart. Then Matty throws one at him and he ducks out o' the way—but swings just the same. Matty must of been wise by this time, for he pitches one so far outside that the Chief almost has to go to the coachers' box after it.

Elliott takes his third healthy and runs through the field down to the clubhouse.

We got beat in the eleventh; and when we went in to dress he has his street clothes on. Soon as he seen John comin' he says: "I got to see McGraw!" And he beat it.

John was goin' to the fights that night; but before he leaves the hotel he had waivers on Elliott from everybody and had sold him to Atlanta.

"And," says John, "I don't care if they pay for him or not." My roomy blows in about nine and got the letter from John out of his box. He was goin' to tear it up. but I told him they was news in it. He opens it and reads where he's sold. I was still sore at him; so I says:

"Thought you was goin' to get on the New York club?"

"No," he says. "I got turned down cold. McGraw says he wouldn't have me in his club. He says he'd had Charlie Faust—and that was enough for him."

He had a kind o' crazy look in his eyes; so when he starts up to the room I follows him.

"What are you goin' to do now?" I says.

"I'm goin' to sell this ticket to Atlanta," he says, "and go back to Muskegon, where I belong."

"I'll help you pack," I says.

"No," says the bug. "I come into this league with this suit o' clothes and a collar. They can have the rest of it." Then he sits dawn on the bed and begins to cry like a baby. "No series dough for me," he blubbers, "and no weddin' bells! My girl'll die when she hears about it!"

Of course that made me feel kind o' rotten, and I says:

"Brace up, boy! The best thing you can do is go to Atlanta and try hard. You'll be up here again next year."

"You can't tell me where to go!" he says, and he wasn't cryin' no more. "I'll go where I please—and I'm li'ble to take you with me."

I didn't want no argument, so I kep' still. Pretty soon he goes up to the lookin'-glass and stares at himself for five minutes. Then, all of a sudden, he hauls off and takes a wallop at his reflection in the glass. Naturally he smashed the glass all to pieces and he cut his hand somethin' awful.

Without lookin' at it he come over to me and says: "Well, good-by, sport!"—and holds out his other hand to shake. When I starts to shake with him he smears his bloody hand all over my map. Then he laughed like a wild man and run out o' the room and out o' the hotel.

VIII

Well, boys, my sleep was broke up for the rest o' the season. It might of been because I was used to sleepin' in all kinds o' racket and excitement, and couldn't stand for the quiet after he'd went—or it might of been because I kep' thinkin' about him and feelin' sorry for him.

I of'en wondered if he'd settle down and be somethin' if he could get married; and finally I got to b'lievin' he would. So when we was dividin' the city series dough I was thinkin' of him and the girl. Our share o' the money—the losers', as usual—was twelve thousand seven hundred sixty bucks or somethin' like that. They was twenty-one of us and that meant six hundred seven bucks apiece. We was just goin' to cut it up that way when I says:

"Why not give a divvy to poor old Elliott?"

About fifteen of 'em at once told me that I was crazy. You see, when he got canned he owed everybody in the club. I guess he'd stuck me for the most—

about seventy bucks—but I didn't care nothin' about that. I knowed he hadn't never reported to Atlanta, and I thought he was prob'ly busted and a bunch o' money might make things all right for him and the other songbird.

I made quite a speech to the fellers, tellin' 'em how he'd cried when he left us and how his heart'd been set on gettin' married on the series dough. I made it so strong that they finally fell for it. Our shares was cut to five hundred eighty apiece, and John sent him a check for a full share.

For a while I was kind o' worried about what I'd did. I didn't know if I was doin' right by the girl to give him the chance to marry her.

He'd told me she was stuck on him, and that's the only excuse I had for tryin' to fix it up between 'em; but, b'lieve me, if she was my sister or a friend o' mine I'd just as soon of had her manage the Cincinnati Club as marry that bird. I thought to myself:

"If she's all right she'll take acid in a month—and it'll be my fault; but if she's really stuck on him they must be somethin' wrong with her too, so what's the diff'rence?"

Then along comes this letter that I told you about. It's from some friend of hisn up there—and they's a note from him. I'll read 'em to you and then I got to beat it for the station:

Dear Sir: They have got poor Elliott locked up and they are goin' to take him to the asylum at Kalamazoo. He thanks you for the cheek, and we will use the money to see that he is made comf'table.

When the poor boy came back here he found that his girl was married to Joe Bishop, who runs a soda fountain. She had wrote to him about it, but he did not read her letters. The news drove him crazy—poor boy—and he went to the place where they was livin' with a baseball bat and very near killed 'em both. Then he marched down the street singin' 'Silver Threads Among the Gold' at the top of his voice. They was goin' to send him to prison for assault with intent to kill, but the jury decided he was crazy.

He wants to thank you again for the money.

Yours truly, Jim—

I can't make out his last name—but it don't make no diff'rence. Now I'll read you his note:

Old Roomy: I was at bat twice and made two hits; but I guess I did not meet 'em square. They tell me they are both alive yet which I did not mean 'em to be. I hope they got good curve-ball pitchers where I am goin'. I sure can bust them curves—can't I, sport?

Yours, B. Elliott.

P.S.—The B stands for Buster.

That's all of it, fellers; and you can see I had same excuse for not hittin'. You can also see why I ain't never goin' to room with no bug again—not for John or nobody else!

Horseshoes

The series ended Tuesday, but I had stayed in Philadelphia an extra day on the chance of there being some follow-up stuff worth sending. Nothing had broken loose; so I filed some stuff about what the Athletics and Giants were going to do with their dough, and then caught the eight o'clock train for Chicago.

Having passed up supper in order to get my story away and grab the train, I went to the buffet car right after I'd planted my grips. I sat down at one of the tables and ordered a sandwich. Four salesmen were playing rum at the other table and all the chairs in the car were occupied; so it didn't surprise me when somebody flopped down in the seat opposite me.

I looked up from my paper and with a little thrill recognized my companion. Now I've been experting round the country with ball players so much that it doesn't usually excite me to meet one face to face, even if he's a star. I can talk with Tyrus without getting all fussed up. But this particular player had jumped from obscurity to fame so suddenly and had played such an important though brief part in the recent argument between the Macks and McGraws that I couldn't help being a little awed by his proximity.

It was none other than Grimes, the utility outfielder Connie had been forced to use in the last game because of the injury to Joyce—Grimes, whose miraculous catch in the eleventh inning had robbed Parker of a home run and the Giants of victory, and whose own homer—a fluky one—had given the Athletics another World's Championship.

I had met Grimes one day during the spring he was with the Cubs, but I knew he wouldn't remember me. A ball player never recalls a reporter's face on less than six introductions or his name on less than twenty. However, I resolved to speak to him, and had just mustered sufficient courage to open a conversation when he saved me the trouble.

"Whose picture have they got there?" he asked, pointing to my paper.

"Speed Parker's," I replied.

"What do they say about him? " asked Grimes. "I'll read it to you," I said:

Speed Parker, McGraw's great third baseman, is ill in a local hospital with nervous prostration, the result of the strain of the World's Series, in which he played such a stellar rle. Parker is in such a dangerous condition that no one is allowed to see him. Members of the New York team and fans from Gotham called at the hospital to-day, but were unable to gain admittance to his ward. Philadelphians hope he will recover speedily and will suffer no permanent ill effects from his sickness, for he won their admiration by his work in the series, though he was on a rival team. A lucky catch by Grimes, the Athletics' substitute outfielder, was all that prevented Parker from winning the title for New York. According to Manager Mack, of the champions, the series would have been over in four games but for Parker's wonderful exhibition of nerve and—"

"That'll be a plenty," Grimes interrupted. "And that's just what you might expect from one o' them doughheaded reporters. If all the baseball writers was where they belonged they'd have to build an annex to Matteawan."

I kept my temper with very little effort—it takes more than a peevish ball player's remarks to insult one of our fraternity; but I didn't exactly understand his peeve.

"Doesn't Parker deserve the bouquet?" I asked.

"Oh, they can boost him all they want to," said Grimes; "but when they call that catch lucky and don't mention the fact that Parker is the luckiest guy in the world, somethin' must be wrong with 'em. Did you see the serious?"

"No," I lied glibly, hoping to draw from him the cause of his grouch.

"Well," he said, "you sure missed somethin'. They never was a serious like it before and they won't never be one again. It went the full seven games and every game was a bear. They was one big innin' every day and Parker was the big cheese in it. Just as Connie says, the Ath-a-letics would of cleaned 'em in four games but for Parker; but it wasn't because he's a great ball player—it was because he was born with a knife, fork and spoon in his mouth, and a rabbit's foot hung round his neck.

"You may not know it, but I'm Grimes, the guy that made the lucky catch. I'm the guy that won the serious with a hit—a home-run hit; and I'm here to tell you that if I'd had one-tenth o' Parker's luck they'd of heard about me long before yesterday. They say my homer was lucky. Maybe it was; but, believe me, it was time things broke for me. They been breakin' for him all his life."

"Well," I said, "his luck must have gone back on him if he's in a hospital with nervous prostration."

"Nervous prostration nothin'," said Grimes. "He's in a hospital because his face is all out o' shape and he's ashamed to appear on the street. I don't usually do so much talkin' and I'm ravin' a little to-night because I've had a couple o' drinks; but—"

"Have another," said I, ringing for the waiter, "and talk some more."

"I made two hits yesterday," Grimes went on, "but the crowd only seen one. I busted up the game and the serious with the one they seen. The one they didn't see was the one I busted up a guy's map with—and

Speed Parker was the guy. That's why he's in a hospital. He may be able to play ball next year; but I'll bet my share o' the dough that McGraw won't reco'nize him when he shows up at Marlin in the spring."

"When did this come off?" I asked. "And why?"

"It come off outside the clubhouse after yesterday's battle," he said; " and I hit him because he called me a name—a name I won't stand for from him."

"What did he call you?" I queried, expecting to hear one of the delicate epithets usually applied by conquered to conqueror on the diamond.

"'Horseshoes!'" was Grimes' amazing reply.

"But, good Lord!" I remonstrated, "I've heard of ball players calling each other that, and Lucky Stiff, and Fourleaf Clover, ever since I was a foot high, and I never knew them to start fights about it."

"Well," said Grimes, "I might as well give you all the dope; and then if you don't think I was justified I'll pay your fare from here to wherever you're goin'. I don't want you to think I'm kickin' about trifles—or that I'm kickin' at all, for that matter. I just want to prove to you that he didn't have no license to pull that Horseshoes stuff on me and that I only give him what was comin' to him."

"Go ahead and shoot," said I.

"Give us some more o' the same," said Grimes to the passing waiter. And then he told me about it.

Maybe you've heard that me and Speed Parker was raised in the same town—Ishpeming, Michigan. We was kids together, and though he done all the devilment I got all the lickin's. When we was about twelve years old Speed throwed a rotten egg at the teacher and I got expelled. That made me sick o' schools and I wouldn't never go to one again, though my ol' man beat me up and the truant officers threatened to have me hung.

Well, while Speed was learnin' what was the principal products o' New Hampshire and Texas I was workin' round the freight-house and drivin' a dray.

We'd both been playin' ball all our lives; and when the town organized a semi-pro club we got jobs with it. We was to draw two bucks apiece for each game and they played every Sunday. We played four games before we got our first pay. They was a hole in my pants pocket as big as the home plate, but I forgot about it and put the dough in there. It wasn't there when I got home. Speed didn't have no hole in his pocket—you can bet on that! Afterward the club hired a good outfielder and I was canned. They was huntin' for another third baseman too; but, o' course, they didn't find none and Speed held his job.

The next year they started the Northern Peninsula League. We landed with the home team. The league opened in May and blowed up the third week in June. They paid off all the outsiders first and then had just money enough left to settle with one of us two Ishpeming guys. The night they done the payin' I was out to my uncle's farm, so they settled with Speed and told me I'd have to wait for mine. I'm still waitin'!

Gene Higgins, who was manager o' the Battle Creek Club, lived in Houghton, and that winter we goes over and strikes him for a job. He give it to us and we busted in together two years ago last spring.

I had a good year down there. I hit over .300 and stole all the bases in sight. Speed got along good too, and they was several big-league scouts lookin' us over. The Chicago Cubs bought Speed outright and four clubs put in a draft for me. Three of 'em—Cleveland and the New York Giants and the Boston Nationals—needed outfielders bad, and it would of been a pipe for me to of made good with any of 'em. But who do you think got me? The same Chicago Cubs; and the only outfielders they had at that time was Schulte and Leach and Good and Williams and Stewart, and one or two others.

Well, I didn't figure I was any worse off than Speed. The Cubs had Zimmerman at third base and it didn't look like they was any danger of a busher beatin' him out; but Zimmerman goes and breaks his leg the second day o' the season—that's a year ago last April—and Speed jumps right in as a regular. Do you think anything like that could happen to Schulte or Leach, or any o' them outfielders? No, sir! I wore out my uniform slidin' up and down the bench and wonderin' whether they'd ship me to Fort Worth or Siberia.

Now I want to tell you about the miserable luck Speed had right off the reel. We was playin' at St. Louis. They had a one-run lead in the eighth, when their pitcher walked Speed with one out. Saier hits a high fly to centre and Parker starts with the crack o' the bat. Both coachers was yellin' at him to go back, but he thought they was two out and he was clear round to third base when the ball come down. And Oakes muffs it! O' course he scored and the game was tied up.

Parker come in to the bench like he'd did something wonderful.

"Did you think they was two out?" ast Hank.

"No," says Speed, blushin'.

"Then what did you run for?" says Hank.

"I had a hunch he was goin' to drop the ball," says Speed; and Hank pretty near falls off the bench.

The next day he come up with one out and the sacks full, and the score tied in the sixth. He smashes one on the ground straight at Hauser and it looked like a cinch double play; but just as Hauser was goin' to grab it the ball hit a rough spot and hopped a mile over his head. It got between Oakes and Magee and went clear to the fence. Three guys scored and Speed pulled up at third. The papers come out and said the game was won by a three-bagger from the bat o' Parker, the Cubs' sensational kid third baseman. Gosh!

We go home to Chi and are havin' a hot battle with Pittsburgh. This time Speed's turn come when they was two on and two out, and Pittsburgh a run to the good—I think it was the eighth innin'. Cooper gives him a fast one and he hits it straight up in the air. O' course the runners started goin', but it looked hopeless because they wasn't no wind or high sky to bother anybody. Mowrey and Gibson both goes after the ball; and just as Mowrey was set for the catch Gibson bumps into him and they both fall down. Two runs scored and Speed got to second. Then what does he do but try to steal third—with two out too! And Gibson's peg pretty near hits the left field seats on the fly.

When Speed comes to the bench Hank says:

"If I was you I'd quit playin' ball and go to Monte Carlo."

"What for?" says Speed.

"You're so dam' lucky!" says Hank.

"So is Ty Cobb," says Speed. That's how he hated himself!

First trip to Cincy we run into a couple of old Ishpeming boys. They took us out one night, and about twelve o'clock I said we'd have to go back to the hotel or we'd get fined. Speed said I had cold feet and he stuck with the boys. I went back alone and Hank caught me comin' in and put a fifty-dollar plaster on me. Speed stayed out all night long and Hank never knowed it. I says to myself: "Wait till he gets out there and tries to play ball without no sleep!" But the game that day was called off on account o' rain. Can you beat it?

I remember what he got away with the next afternoon the same as though it happened yesterday. In the second innin' they walked him with nobody down, and he took a big lead off first base like he always does. Benton throwed over there three or four times to scare him back, and the last time he throwed, Hobby hid the ball. The coacher seen it and told Speed to hold the bag; but he didn't pay no attention. He started leadin' right off again and Hobby tried to tag him, but the ball slipped out of his hand and rolled about a yard away. Parker had plenty o' time to get back; but, instead o' that, he starts for second. Hobby picked up the ball and shot it down to Groh—and Groh made a square muff.

Parker slides into the bag safe and then gets up and throws out his chest like he'd made the greatest play ever. When the ball's throwed back to Benton, Speed leads off about thirty foot and stands there in a trance. Clarke signs for a pitch-out and pegs down to second to nip him. He was caught flatfooted—that is, he would of been with a decent throw; but Clarke's peg went pretty near to Latonia. Speed scored and strutted over to receive our hearty congratulations. Some o' the boys was laughin' and he thought they was laughin' with him instead of at him.

It was in the ninth, though, that he got by with one o' the worst I ever seen. The Reds was a run behind and Marsans was on third base with two out. Hobby, I think it was, hit one on the ground right at Speed and he picked it up clean. The crowd all got up and started for the exits. Marsans run toward the plate in the faint hope that the peg to first would be wild. All of a sudden the boys on the Cincy bench begun yellin' at him to slide, and he done so. He was way past the plate when Speed's throw got to Archer. The bonehead had shot the ball home instead o' to first base, thinkin' they was only one down. We was all crazy, believin' his nut play had let 'em tie it up; but he comes tearin' in, tellin' Archer to tag Marsans. So Jim walks over and tags the Cuban, who was brushin' off his uniform.

"You're out!" says Klem. "You never touched the plate."

I guess Marsans knowed the umps was right because he didn't make much of a holler. But Speed sure got a pannin' in the club-house.

"I suppose you knowed he was goin' to miss the plate!" says Hank sarcastic as he could.

Everybody on the club roasted him, but it didn't do no good.

Well, you know what happened to me. I only got into one game with the Cubs—one afternoon when Leach was sick. We was playin' the Boston bunch and Tyler was workin' against us. I always had trouble with lefthanders and this was one of his good days. I couldn't see what he throwed up there. I got one foul durin' the afternoon's entertainment; and the wind was blowin' a hundred-mile gale, so that the best outfielder in the world couldn't judge a fly ball. That Boston bunch must of hit fifty of 'em and they all come to my field.

If I caught any I've forgot about it. Couple o' days after that I got notice o' my release to Indianapolis.

Parker kept right on all season doin' the blamnedest things you ever heard of and gettin' by with 'em. One o' the boys told me about it later. If they was playin' a double-header in St. Louis, with the thermometer at 130 degrees, he'd get put out by the umps in the first innin' o' the first game. If he started to steal the catcher'd drop the pitch or somebody'd muff the throw. If he hit a pop fly the sun'd get in somebody's eyes. If he took a swell third strike with the bases full the umps would call it a ball. If he cut first base by twenty feet the umps would be readin' the mornin' paper.

Zimmerman's leg mended, so that he was all right by June; and then Saier got sick and they tried Speed at first base. He'd never saw the bag before; but things kept on breakin' for him and he played it like a house afire. The Cubs copped the pennant and Speed got in on the big dough, besides playin' a whale of a game through the whole serious.

Speed and me both went back to Ishpeming to spend the winter—though the Lord knows it ain't no winter resort. Our homes was there; and besides, in my case, they was a certain girl livin' in the old burg.

Parker, o' course, was the hero and the swell guy when we got home. He'd been in the World's Serious and had plenty o' dough in his kick. I come home with nothin' but my suitcase and a hard-luck story, which I kept to myself. I hadn't even went good enough in Indianapolis to be sure of a job there again.

That fall—last fall—an uncle o' Speed's died over in the Soo and left him ten thousand bucks. I had an uncle down in the Lower Peninsula who was worth five times that much—but he had good health!

This girl I spoke about was the prettiest thing I ever see. I'd went with her in the old days, and when I blew back I found she was still strong for me. They wasn't a great deal o' variety in Ishpeming for a girl to pick from. Her and I went to the dance every Saturday night and to church Sunday nights. I called on her Wednesday evenin's, besides takin' her to all the shows that come along—rotten as the most o' them was.

I never knowed Speed was makin' a play for this doll till along last Feb'uary. The minute I seen what was up I got busy. I took her out sleigh-ridin' and kept her out in the cold till she'd promised to marry me. We set the date for this fall—I figured I'd know better where I was at by that time.

Well, we didn't make no secret o' bein' engaged; down in the poolroom one night Speed come up and congratulated me. He says:

"You got a swell girl, Dick! I wouldn't mind bein' in your place. You're mighty lucky to cop her out—you old Horseshoes, you!"

"Horseshoes!" I says. "You got a fine license to call anybody Horseshoes! I suppose you ain't never had no luck?"

"Not like you," he says.

I was feelin' too good about grabbin' the girl to get sore at the time; but when I got to thinkin' about it a few minutes afterward it made me mad clear through. What right did that bird have to talk about me bein' lucky?

Speed was playin' freeze-out at a table near the door, and when I started home some o' the boys with him says:

"Good night, Dick."

I said good night and then Speed looked up.

"Good night, Horseshoes!" he says.

That got my nanny this time.

"Shut up, you lucky stiff!" I says. "If you wasn't so dam' lucky you'd be sweepin' the streets." Then I walks on out.

I was too busy with the girl to see much o' Speed after that. He left home about the middle o' the month to go to Tampa with the Cubs. I got notice from Indianapolis that I was sold to Baltimore. I didn't care much about goin' there and I wasn't anxious to leave home under the circumstances, so I didn't report till late.

When I read in the papers along in April that Speed had been traded to Boston for a couple o' pitchers I thought: "Gee! He must of lost his rabbit's foot!" Because, even if the Cubs didn't cop again, they'd have a city serious with the White Sox and get a bunch o' dough that way. And they wasn't no chance in the world for the Boston Club to get nothin' but their salaries.

It wasn't another month, though, till Shafer, o' the Giants, quit baseball and McGraw was up against it for a third baseman. Next thing I knowed Speed was traded to New York and was with another winner—for they never was out o' first place all season.

I was gettin' along all right at Baltimore and Dunnie liked me; so I felt like I had somethin' more than just a one-year job—somethin' I could get married on. It was all framed that the weddin' was comin' off as soon as this season was over; so you can believe I was pullin' for October to hurry up and come.

One day in August, two months ago, Dunnie come in the club-house and handed me the news.

"Rube Oldring's busted his leg," he says, "and he's out for the rest o' the season. Connie's got a youngster named Joyce that he can stick in there, but he's got to have an extra outfielder. He's made me a good proposition for you and I'm goin' to let you go. It'll be pretty soft for yQu, because they got the pennant cinched and they'll cut you in on the big money."

"Yes," I says; "and when they're through with me they'll ship me to Hellangone, and I'll be draggin' down about seventy-five bucks a month next year."

"Nothin' like that," says Dunnie. "If he don't want you next season he's got to ask for waivers; and if you get out o' the big league you come right back here. That's all framed."

So that's how I come to get with the Ath-a-letics. Connie give me a nice, comf'table seat in one corner o' the bench and I had the pleasure o' watchin' a real ball club perform once every afternoon and sometimes twice.

Connie told me that as soon as they had the flag cinched he was goin' to lay off some o' his regulars and I'd get a chance to play.

Well, they cinched it the fourth day o' September and our next engagement was with Washin'ton on Labor Day. We had two games and I was in both of 'em. And I broke in with my usual lovely luck, because the pitchers I was ast to face was Boehling, a nasty lefthander, and this guy Johnson.

The mornin' game was Boebling's and he wasn't no worse than some o' the rest of his kind. I only whiffed once and would of had a triple if Milan hadn't run from here to New Orleans and stole one off me.

I'm not boastin' about my first experience with Johnson though. They can't never tell me he throws them balls with his arm. He's got a gun concealed about his person and he shoots 'em up there. I was leadin' off in Murphy's place and the game was a little delayed in startin', because I'd watched the big guy warm up and wasn't in no hurry to get to that plate. Before I left the bench Connie says:

Don't try to take no healthy swing. Just meet 'em and you'll get a long better."

So I tried to just meet the first one he throwed; but when I stuck out my bat Henry was throwin' the pill back to Johnson. Then I thought Maybe if I start swingin' now at the second one I'll hit the third one. So I let the second one come over and the umps guessed it was another strike, though I'll bet a thousand bucks he couldn't see it no more'n I could.

While Johnson was still windin' up to pitch again I started to swing—and the big cuss crosses me with a slow one. I lunged at it twice and missed it both times, and the force o' my wallop throwed me clean back to the bench. The Ath-a-letics was all laughin' at me and I laughed too, because I was glad that much of it was over.

McInnes gets a base hit off him in the second innin' and I ast him how he done it.

"He's a friend o' mine," says Jack, "and he lets up when he pitches to me."

I made up my mind right there that if I was goin' to be in the league next year I'd go out and visit Johnson this winter and get acquainted.

I wished before the day was over that I was hittin' in the catcher's place, because the fellers down near the tail-end of the battin' order only had to face him three times. He fanned me on three pitched balls again in the third, and when I come up in the sixth he scared me to death by pretty near beanin' me with the first one.

"Be careful!" says Henry. "He's gettin' pretty wild and he's liable to knock you away from your uniform."

"Don't he never curve one?" I ast.

"Sure!" says Henry. "Do you want to see his curve?"

"Yes," I says, knowin' the hook couldn't be no worse'n the fast one.

So he give me three hooks in succession and I missed 'em all; but I felt more comf'table than when I was duckin' his fast ball. In the ninth he hit my bat with a curve and the ball went on the ground to McBride. He booted it, but throwed me out easy—because I was so surprised at not havin' whiffed that I forgot to run!

Well, I went along like that for the rest o' the season, runnin' up against the best pitchers in the league and not exactly murderin' 'em. Everything I tried went wrong, and I was smart enough to know that if anything had depended on the games I wouldn't of been in there for two minutes. Joyce and Strunk and Murphy wasn't jealous o' me a bit; but they was glad to take turns restin', and I didn't care much how I went so long as I was sure of a job next year.

I'd wrote to the girl a couple o' times askin' her to set the exact date for our weddin'; but she hadn't paid no attention. She said she was glad I was with the Ath-a-letics, but she thought the Giants was goin' to beat us. I might of suspected from that that somethin' was wrong, because not even a girl would pick the Giants to trim that bunch of ourn. Finally, the day before the serious started, I sent her a kind o' sassy letter sayin' I guessed it was up to me to name the day, and askin' whether October twentieth was all right. I told her to wire me yes or no.

I'd been readin' the dope about Speed all season, and I knowed he'd had a whale of a year and that his luck was right with him; but I never dreamed a man could have the Lord on his side as strong as Speed did in that World's Serious! I might as well tell you all the dope, so long as you wasn't there.

The first game was on our grounds and Connie give us a talkin' to in the clubhouse beforehand.

"The shorter this serious is," he says, "the better for us. If it's a long serious we're goin' to have trouble, because McGraw's got five pitchers he can work and we've got about three; so I want you boys to go at 'em from the jump and play 'em off their feet. Don't take things easy, because it ain't goin' to be no snap. Just because we've licked 'em before ain't no sign we'll do it this time."

Then he calls me to one side and ast me what I knowed about Parker.

"You was with the Cubs when he was, wasn't you?" he says.

"Yes," I says; "and he's the luckiest stiff you ever seen! If he got stewed and fell in the gutter he'd catch a fish."

"I don't like to hear a good ball player called lucky," says Connie. "He must have a lot of ability or McGraw wouldn't use him regular. And he's been hittin' about .340 and played a hang-up game at third base. That can't be all luck."

"Wait till you see him," I says; "and if you don't say he's the luckiest guy in the world you can sell me to the Boston Bloomer Girls. He's so lucky," I says, "that if they traded him to the St. Louis Browns they'd have the pennant cinched by the Fourth o' July."

And I'll bet Connie was willin' to agree with me before it was over.

Well, the Chief worked against the Big Rube in that game. We beat 'em, but they give us a battle and it was Parker that made it close. We'd gone along nothin' and nothin' till the seventh, and then Rube walks Collins and Baker lifts one over that little old wall. You'd think by this time them New York pitchers would know better than to give that guy anything he can hit.

In their part o' the ninth the Chief still had 'em shut out and two down, and the crowd was goin' home; but Doyle gets hit in the sleeve with a pitched ball and it's Speed's turn. He hits a foul pretty near straight up, but Schang misjudges it. Then he lifts another one and this time McInnes drops it. He'd ought to of been out twice. The Chief tries to make him hit at a bad one then, because he'd got him two strikes and nothin'. He hit at it all right—kissed it for three bases between Strunk and Joyce! And it was a wild pitch that he hit. Doyle scores, o' course, and the bugs suddenly decide not to go home just yet. I fully expected to see him steal home and get away with it, but Murray cut into the first ball and lined out to Barry.

Plank beat Matty two to one the next day in New York, and again Speed and his rabbit's foot give us an awful argument. Matty wasn't so good as usual and we really ought to of beat him bad. Two different times Strunk was on second waitin' for any kind o' wallop, and both times Barry cracked 'em down the third-base line like a shot. Speed stopped the first one with his stomach and extricated the pill just in time to nail Barry at first base and retire the side. The next time he throwed his glove in front of his face in self-defense and the ball stuck in it.

In the sixth innin' Schang was on third base and Plank on first, and two down, and Murphy combed an awful one to Speed's left. He didn't have time to stoop over and he just stuck out his foot. The ball hit it and caromed in two hops right into Doyle's hands on second base before Plank got there. Then in the seventh Speed bunts one and Baker trips and falls goin' after it or he'd of threw him out a mile. They was two gone; so Speed steals second, and, o' course, Schang has to make a bad peg right at that time and lets him go to third. Then Collins boots one on Murray and they've got a run. But it didn't do 'em no good, because Collins and Baker and McInnes come up in the ninth and walloped 'em where Parker couldn't reach 'em.

Comin' back to Philly on the train that night, I says to Connie:

"What do you think o' that Parker bird now?"

"He's lucky, all right," says Connie smilin'; "but we won't hold it against him if he don't beat us with it."

"It ain't too late," I says. "He ain't pulled his real stuff yet."

The whole bunch was talkin' about him and his luck, and sayin' it was about time for things to break against him. I warned 'em that they wasn't no chance— that it was permanent with him.

Bush and Tesreau hooked up next day and neither o' them had much stuff. Everybody was hittin' and it looked like anybody's game right up to the ninth. Speed had got on every time he come up—the wind blowin' his fly balls away from the outfielders and the infielders bootin' when he hit 'em on the ground.

When the ninth started the score was seven apiece. Connie and McGraw both had their whole pitchin' staffs warmin' up. The crowd was wild, because they'd been all kinds of action. They wasn't no danger of anybody's leavin' their seats before this game was over.

Well, Bescher is walked to start with and Connie's about ready to give Bush one hook; but Doyle pops out tryin' to bunt. Then Speed gets two strikes and two balls, and it looked to me like the next one was right over the heart; but Connolly calls it a ball and gives him another chance. He whales the groove ball to the fence in left center and gets round to third on it, while Bescher scores. Right then Bush comes out and the Chief goes in. He whiffs Murray and has two strikes on Merkle when Speed makes a break for home—and, o' course, that was the one ball Schang dropped in the whole serious!

They had a two-run lead on us then and it looked like a cinch for them to hold it, because the minute Tesreau showed a sign o' weakenin' McGraw was sure to holler for Matty or the Rube. But you know how quick that bunch of ourn can make a two-run lead look sick. Before McGraw could get Jeff out o' there we had two on the bases.

Then Rube comes in and fills 'em up by walkin' Joyce. It was Eddie's turn to wallop and if he didn't do nothin' we had Baker comin' up next. This time Collins saved Baker the trouble and whanged one clear to the woods. Everybody scored but him—and he could of, too, if it'd been necessary.

In the clubhouse the boys naturally felt pretty good. We'd copped three in a row and it looked like we'd make it four straight, because we had the Chief to send back at 'em the followin' day.

"Your friend Parker is lucky," the boys says to me, "but it don't look like he could stop us now."

I felt the same way and was consultin' the time-tables to see whether I could get a train out o' New York for the West next evenin'. But do you think Speed's luck was ready to quit? Not yet! And it's a wonder we didn't all go nuts durin' the next few days. If words could kill, Speed would of died a thousand times. And I wish he had!

They wasn't no record-breakin' crowd out when we got to the Polo Grounds. I guess the New York bugs was pretty well discouraged and the bettin' was eight to five that we'd cop that battle and finish it. The Chief was the only guy that warmed up for us and McGraw didn't have no choice but to use Matty, with the whole thing dependin' on this game.

They went along like the two swell pitchers they was till Speed's innin', which in this battle was the eighth. Nobody scored, and it didn't look like they was ever goin' to till Murphy starts off that round with a perfect bunt and Joyce sacrifices him to second. All

Matty had to do then was to get rid o' Collins and Baker—and that's about as easy as sellin' silk socks to an Eskimo.

He didn't give Eddie nothin' he wanted to hit, though; and finally he slaps one on the ground to Doyle. Larry made the play to first base and Murphy moved to third. We all figured Matty'd walk Baker then, and he done it. Connie sends Baker down to second on the first pitch to McInnes, but Meyers don't pay no attention to him—they was playin' for McInnes and wasn't takin' no chances o' throwin' the ball away.

Well, the count goes to three and two on McInnes and Matty comes with a curve—he's got some curve too; but Jack happened to meet it and—Blooie! Down the left foul line where he always hits! I never seen a ball hit so hard in my life. No infielder in the world could of stopped it. But I'll give you a thousand bucks if that ball didn't go kerplunk right into the third bag and stop as dead as George Washington! It was child's play for Speed to pick it up and heave it over to Merkle before Jack got there. If anybody else had been playin' third base the bag would of ducked out o' the way o' that wallop; but even the bases themselves was helpin' him out.

The two runs we ought to of had on Jack's smash would of been just enough to beat 'em, because they got the only run o' the game in their half—or, I should say, the Lord give it to 'em.

Doyle'd been throwed out and up come Parker, smilin'. The minute I seen him smile I felt like somethin' was comin' off and I made the remark on the bench.

Well, the Chief pitched one right at him and he tried to duck. The ball hit his bat and went on a line between Jack and Eddie. Speed didn't know he'd hit it till the guys on the bench wised him up. Then he just had time to get to first base. They tried the hit-and-run on the second ball and Murray lifts a high fly that Murphy didn't have to move for. Collins pulled the old bluff about the ball bein' on the ground and Barry yells, "Go on! Go on!" like he was the coacher. Speed fell for it and didn't know where the ball was no more'n a rabbit; he just run his fool head off and we was gettin' all ready to laugh when the ball come down and Murphy dropped it!

If Parker had stuck near first base, like he ought to of done, he couldn't of got no farther'n second; but with the start he got he was pretty near third when Murphy made the muff, and it was a cinch for him to score. The next two guys was easy outs; so they wouldn't of had a run except for Speed's boner. We couldn't do nothin' in the ninth and we was licked.

Well, that was a tough one to lose; but we figured that Matty was through and we'd wind it up the next day, as we had Plank ready to send back at 'em. We wasn't afraid o' the Rube, because he hadn't never bothered Collins and Baker much.

The two lefthanders come together just like everybody'd doped it and it was about even up to the eighth. Plank had been goin' great and, though the score was two and two, they'd got their two on boots and we'd hit ourn in. We went after Rube in our part o' the eighth and knocked him out. Demaree stopped us after we'd scored two more.

"It's all over but the shoutin'!" says Davis on the bench.

"Yes," I says, "unless that seventh son of a seventh son gets up there again."

He did, and he come up after they'd filled the bases with a boot, a base hit and a walk with two out. I says to Davis:

"If I was Plank I'd pass him and give 'em one run."

"That wouldn't be no baseball," says Davis—"not with Murray comin' up."

Well, it mayn't of been no baseball, but it couldn't of turned out worse if they'd did it that way. Speed took a healthy at the first ball; but it was a hook and he caught it on the handle, right up near his hands. It started outside the first-base line like a foul and then changed its mind and rolled in. Schang run away from the plate, because it looked like it was up to him to make the play. He picked the ball up and had to make the peg in a hurry.

His throw hit Speed right on top o' the head and bounded off like it had struck a cement sidewalk. It went clear over to the seats and before McInnes could get it three guys had scored and Speed was on third base. He was left there, but that didn't make no difference. We was licked again and for the first time the gang really begun to get scared.

We went over to New York Sunday afternoon and we didn't do no singin' on the way. Some o' the fellers tried to laugh, but it hurt 'em. Connie sent us to bed early, but I don't believe none o' the bunch got much sleep—I know I didn't; I was worryin' too much about the serious and also about the girl, who hadn't sent me no telegram like I'd ast her to. Monday mornin' I wired her askin' what was the matter and tellin' her I was gettin' tired of her foolishness. O' course I didn't make it so strong as that—but the telegram cost me a dollar and forty cents.

Connie had the choice o' two pitchers for the sixth game. He could use Bush, who'd been slammed round pretty hard last time out, or the Chief, who'd only had two days' rest. The rest of 'em—outside o' Plank—had a epidemic o' sore arms. Connie finally picked Bush, so's he could have the Chief in reserve in case we had to play a seventh game. McGraw started Big Jeff and we went at it.

It wasn't like the last time these two guys had hooked up. This time they both had somethin', and for eight innin's runs was as scarce as Chinese policemen. They'd been chances to score on both sides, but the big guy and Bush was both tight in the pinches. The crowd was plumb nuts and yelled like Indians every time a fly ball was caught or a strike called. They'd of got their money's worth if they hadn't been no ninth; but, believe me, that was some round!

They was one out when Barry hit one through the box for a base. Schang walked, and it was Bush's turn. Connie told him to bunt, but he whiffed in the attempt. Then Murphy comes up and walks—and the bases are choked. Young Joyce had been pie for Tesreau all day or else McGraw might of changed pitchers right there. Anyway he left Big Jeff in and he beaned Joyce with a fast one. It sounded like a tire blowin' out. Joyce falls over in a heap and we chase out there, thinkin' he's dead; but he ain't, and pretty soon he gets up and walks down to first base. Tesreau had forced in a run and again we begun to count the winner's end. Matty comes in to prevent further damage and Collins flies the side out.

"Hold 'em now! Work hard!" we says to young Bush, and he walks out there just as cool as though he was goin' to hit fungoes.

McGraw sends up a pinch hitter for Matty and Bush whiffed him. Then Bescher flied out. I was pray-in' that Doyle would end it, because Speed's turn come after his'n; so I pretty near fell dead when Larry hit safe.

Speed had his old smile and even more chest than usual when he come up there, swingin' five or six bats. He didn't wait for Doyle to try and steal, or nothin'. He lit into the first ball, though Bush was tryin' to waste it. I seen the ball go high in the air toward left field, and then I picked up my glove and got ready to beat it for the gate. But when I looked out to see if Joyce was set, what do you think I seen? He was lyin' flat on the ground! That blow on the head had got him just as Bush was pitchin' to Speed. He'd flopped over and didn't no more know what was goin' on than if he'd croaked.

Well, everybody else seen it at the same time; but it was too late. Strunk made a run for the ball, but they wasn't no chance for him to get near it. It hit the ground about ten feet back o' where Joyce was lyin' and bounded way over to the end o' the foul line. You don't have to be told that Doyle and Parker both scored and the serious was tied up.

We carried Joyce to the clubhouse and after a while he come to. He cried when he found out what had happened. We cheered him up all we could, but he was a pretty sick guy. The trainer said he'd be all right, though, for the final game.

They tossed up a coin to see where they'd play the seventh battle and our club won the toss; so we went back to Philly that night and cussed Parker clear across New Jersey. I was so sore I kicked the stuffin' out o' my seat.

You probably heard about the excitement in the burg yesterday mornin'. The demand for tickets was somethin' fierce and some of 'em sold for as high as twenty-five bucks apiece. Our club hadn't been lookin' for no seventh game and they was some tall hustlin' done round that old ball park.

I started out to the grounds early and bought some New York papers to read on the car. They was a big story that Speed Parker, the Giants' hero, was goin' to be married a week after the end o' the serious. It didn't give the name o' the girl, sayin' Speed had refused to tell it. I figured she must be some dame he'd met round the circuit somewheres.

They was another story by one o' them smart baseball reporters sayin' that Parker, on his way up to the plate, had saw that Joyce was about ready to faint and had hit the fly ball to left field on purpose. Can you beat it?

I was goin' to show that to the boys in the clubhouse, but the minute I blowed in there I got some news that made me forget about everything else. Joyce was very sick and they'd took him to a hospital. It was up to me to play!

Connie come over and ast me whether I'd ever hit against Matty. I told him I hadn't, but I'd saw enough of him to know he wasn't no worse'n Johnson. He told me he was goin' to let me hit second—in Joyce's place—because he didn't want to bust up the rest of his combination. He also told me to take my orders from Strunk about where to play for the batters.

"Where shall I play for Parker?" I says, tryin' to joke and pretend I wasn't scared to death.

"I wisht I could tell you," says Connie. "I guess the only thing to do when he comes up is to get down on your knees and pray."

The rest o' the bunch slapped me on the back and give me all the encouragement they could. The place was jammed when we went out on the field. They may of been bigger crowds before, but they never was packed together so tight. I doubt whether they was even room enough left for Falkenberg to sit down.

The afternoon papers had printed the stuff about Joyce bein' out of it, so the bugs was wise that I was goin' to play. They watched me pretty close in battin' practice and give me a hand whenever I managed to hit one hard. When I was out catchin' fungoes the guys in the bleachers cheered me and told me they was with me; but I don't mind tellin' you that I was as nervous as a bride.

They wasn't no need for the announcers to tip the crowd off to the pitchers. Everybody in the United States and Cuba knowed that the Chief'd work for us and Matty for them. The Chief didn't have no trouble with 'em in the first innin'. Even from where I stood I could see that he had a lot o' stuff. Bescher and Doyle popped out and Speed whiffed.

Well, I started out makin' good, with reverse English, in our part. Fletcher booted Murphy's ground ball and I was sent up to sacrifice. I done a complete job of it—sacrificin' not only myself but Murphy with a pop fly that Matty didn't have to move for. That spoiled whatever chance we had o' gettin' the jump on 'em; but the boys didn't bawl me for it.

"That's all right, old boy. You're all right! " they said on the bench—if they'd had a gun they'd of shot me.

I didn't drop no fly balls in the first six innin's—because none was hit out my way. The Chief was so good that they wasn't hittin' nothin' out o' the infield. And we wasn't doin' nothin' with Matty, either. I led off in the fourth and fouled the first one. I didn't molest the other two. But if Connie and the gang talked about me they done it internally. I come up again—with Murphy on third base and two gone in the sixth, and done my little whiffin' specialty. And still the only people that panned me was the thirty thousand that had paid for the privilege!

My first fieldin' chance come in the seventh. You'd of thought that I'd of had my nerve back by that time; but I was just as scared as though I'd never saw a crowd before. It was just as well that they was two out when Merkle hit one to me. I staggered under it and finally it hit me on the shoulder. Merkle got to second, but the

Chief whiffed the next guy. I was gave some cross looks on the bench and I shouldn't of blamed the fellers if they'd cut loose with some language; but they didn't.

They's no use in me tellin' you about none o' the rest of it—except what happened just before the start o' the eleventh and durin' that innin', which was sure the big one o' yesterday's pastime—both for Speed and yours sincerely.

The scoreboard was still a row o' ciphers and Speed'd had only a fair amount o' luck. He'd made a scratch base hit and robbed our bunch of a couple o' real ones with impossible stops.

When Schang flied out and wound up our tenth I was leanin' against the end of our bench. I heard my name spoke, and I turned round and seen a boy at the door.

"Right here!" I says; and he give me a telegram.

"Better not open it till after the game," says Connie.

"Oh, no; it ain't no bad news," I said, for I figured it was an answer from the girl. So I opened it up and read it on the way to my position. It said:

"*Forgive me, Dick—and forgive Speed too. Letter follows.*"

Well, sir, I ain't no baby, but for a minute I just wanted to sit down and bawl. And then, all of a sudden, I got so mad I couldn't see. I run right into Baker as he was pickin' up his glove. Then I give him a shove and called him some name, and him and Barry both looked at me like I was crazy—and I was. When I got out in left field I stepped on my own foot and spiked it. I just had to hurt somebody.

As I remember it the Chief fanned the first two of 'em. Then Doyle catches one just right and lams it up against the fence back o' Murphy. The ball caromed round some and Doyle got all the way to third base. Next thing I seen was Speed struttin' up to the plate. I run clear in from my position.

"Kill him!" I says to the Chief. "Hit him in the head and kill him, and I'll go to jail for it!"

"Are you off your nut?" says the Chief. "Go out there and play ball—and quit ravin.'"

Barry and Baker led me away and give me a shove out toward left. Then I heard the crack o' the bat and I seen the ball comin' a mile a minute. It was headed between Strunk and I and looked like it would go out o' the park. I don't remember runnin' or nothin' about it till I run into the concrete wall head first. They told me afterward and all the papers said that it was the greatest catch ever seen. And I never knowed I'd caught the ball!

Some o' the managers have said my head was pretty hard, but it wasn't as hard as that concrete. I was pretty near out, but they tell me I walked to the bench like I wasn't hurt at all. They also tell me that the crowd was a bunch o' ravin' maniacs and was throwin' money at me. I guess the ground-keeper'll get it.

The boys on the bench was all talkin' at once and slappin' me on the back, but I didn't know what it was about. Somebody told me pretty soon that it was my turn to hit and I picked up the first bat I come to and starts for the plate. McInnes come runnin' after me and ast me whether I didn't want my own bat. I cussed him and told him to mind his own business.

I didn't know it at the time, but I found out afterward that they was two out. The bases was empty. I'll tell you just what I had in my mind: I wasn't thinkin' about the ball game; I was determined that I was goin' to get to third base and give that guy my spikes. If I didn't hit one worth three bases, or if I didn't hit one at all, I was goin' to run till I got round to where Speed was, and then slide into him and cut him to pieces!

Right now I can't tell you whether I hit a fast ball, or a slow ball, or a hook, or a fader—but I hit somethin'. It went over Bescher's head like a shot and then took a crazy bound. It must of struck a rock or a pop bottle, because it hopped clear over the fence and landed in the bleachers.

Mind you, I learned this afterward. At the time I just knowed I'd hit one somewheres and I starts round the bases. I speeded up when I got near third and took a runnin' jump at a guy I thought was Parker. I missed him and sprawled all over the bag. Then, all of a sudden, I come to my senses. All the Ath-a-letics was out there to run home with me and it was one o' them I'd tried to cut. Speed had left the field. The boys picked me up and seen to it that I went on and touched the plate. Then I was carried into the clubhouse by the crazy bugs.

Well, they had a celebration in there and it was a long time before I got a chance to change my clothes. The boys made a big fuss over me. They told me they'd intended to give me five hundred bucks for my divvy, but now I was goin' to get a full share.

"Parker ain't the only lucky guy!" says one of 'em. "But even if that ball hadn't of took that crazy hop you'd of had a triple."

A triple! That's just what I'd wanted; and he called me lucky for not gettin' it!

The Giants was dressin' in the other part o' the clubhouse; and when I finally come out there was Speed, standin' waitin' for some o' the others. He seen me comin' and he smiled. " Hello, Horseshoes!"he says.

He won't smile no more for a while—it'll hurt too much. And if any girl wants him when she sees him now—with his nose over shakin' hands with his ear, and his jaw a couple o' feet foul—she's welcome to him. They won't be no contest!

Grimes leaned over to ring for the waiter.

"Well," he said, "what about it?"

"You won't have to pay my fare," I told him.

"I'll buy a drink anyway," said he. "You've been a good listener—and I had to get it off my chest."

"Maybe they'll have to postpone the wedding," I said.

"No," said Grimes. "The weddin' will take place the day after tomorrow—and I'll bat for Mr. Parker. Did you think I was goin' to let him get away with it?"

"What about next year?" I asked.

"I'm goin' back to the Ath-a-letics," he said. "And I'm goin' to hire somebody to call me 'Horseshoes!' before every game—because I can sure play that old baseball when I'm mad."

Harmony

Even a baseball writer must sometimes work. Regretfully I yielded my seat in the P. G., walked past the section where Art Graham, Bill Cole, Lefty Paiks and young Waldron were giving expert tonsorial treatment to "Sweet Adeline," and flopped down beside Ryan, the manager.

"Well, Cap," I said, "we're due in Springfield in a little over an hour and I haven't written a line."

"Don't let me stop you," said Ryan.

"I want you to start me," I said. "Lord!" said Ryan. "You oughtn't to have any trouble rinding out stuff these days, with the club in first place and young Waldron gone crazy. He's worth a story any day."

"That's the trouble," said I. "He's been worked so much that there's nothing more to say about him. Everybody in the country knows that he's hitting .420, that he's made nine home runs, twelve triples and twenty-some doubles, that he's stolen twenty-five bases, and that he can play the piano and sing like Carus'. They've run his picture oftener than Billy Sunday and Mary Pickford put together. Of course, you might come through with how you got him."

"Oh, that's the mystery," said Ryan.

"So I've heard you say," I retorted. "But it wouldn't be a mystery if you'd let me print it."

"Well," said Ryan, "if you're really hard up I suppose I might as well come through. Only there's really no mystery at all about it; it's just what I consider the most remarkable piece of scouting ever done. I've been making a mystery of it just to have a little fun with Dick Hodges. You know he's got the Jackson club and he's still so sore about my stealing Waldron he'll hardly speak to me.

"I'll give you the dope if you want it, though it's a boost for Art Graham, not me . There's lots of people think the reason I've kept the thing a secret is because I'm modest.

"They give me credit for having found Waldron myself. But Graham is the bird that deserves the credit and I'll admit that he almost had to get down on his knees to make me take his tip. Yes, sir, Art Graham was the scout, and now he's sitting on the bench and the boy he recommended has got his place."

"That sounds pretty good," I said. "And how did Graham get wise?"

"I'm going to tell you. You're in a hurry; so I'll make it snappy.

"You weren't with us last fall, were you? Well, we had a day off in Detroit, along late in the season. Graham's got relatives in Jackson; so he asked me if he could spend the day there. I told him he could and asked him to keep his eyes peeled for good young pitchers, if he happened to go to the ball game. So he went to Jackson and the next morning he came back all excited. I asked him if he'd found me a pitcher and he said he hadn't, but he'd seen the best natural hitter he'd ever looked at—a kid named Waldron.

"'Well,' I said, 'you're the last one that ought to be recommending outfielders. If there's one good enough to hold a regular job, it might be your job he'd get.'

"But Art said that didn't make any difference to him—he was looking out for the good of the club. Well, I didn't see my way clear to asking the old man to dig up good money for an outfielder nobody'd ever heard of, when we were pretty well stocked with them, so I tried to stall Art; but he kept after me and kept after me till I agreed to stick in a draft for the kid just to keep Art quiet. So the draft went in and we got him. Then, as you know, Hodges tried to get him back, and that made me suspicious enough to hold on to him. Hodges finally came over to see me and wanted to know who'd tipped me to Waldron. That's where the mystery stuff started, because I saw that Hodges was all heated up and wanted to kid him along. So I told him we had some mighty good scouts working for us, and he said he knew our regular scouts and they couldn't tell a ball-player from a torn ligament.

Then he offered me fifty bucks if I'd tell him the truth and I just laughed at him. I said: 'A fella happened to be in Jackson one day and saw him work. But I won't tell you who the fella was, because you're too anxious to know.' Then he insisted on knowing what day the scout had been in Jackson. I said I'd tell him that if he'd tell me why he was so blame curious. So he gave me his end of it.

"It seems his brother, up in Ludington, had seen this kid play ball on the lots and had signed him right up for Hodges and taken him to Jackson, and of course, Hodges knew he had a world beater the minute he saw him. But he also knew he wasn't going to be able to keep him in Jackson, and, naturally he began to figure how he could get the most money for him. It was already August when the boy landed in Jackson; so there wasn't much chance of getting a big price last season. He decided to teach the kid what he didn't know about baseball and to keep him under cover till this year. Then everybody would be touting him and there'd be plenty of competition. Hodges could sell to the highest bidder.

"He had Waidron out practising every day, but wouldn't let him play in a game, and every player on the Jackson club had promised to keep the secret till this year. So Hodges wanted to find out from me which one of his players had broken the promise.

"Then I asked him if he was perfectly sure that Waldron hadn't played in a game, and he said he had gone in to hit for somebody just once. I asked him what date that was and he told me. It was the day Art had been in Jackson. So I said:

"'There's your mystery solved. That's the day my scout saw him, and you'll have to give the scout a little credit for picking a star after seeing him make one base hit.'

"Then Hodges said:

"'That makes it all the more a mystery. Because, in the first place, he batted under a fake name. And, in the second place, he didn't make a base hit. He popped out.'

"That's about all there is to it. You can ask Art how he picked the kid out for a star from seeing him pop out once. I've asked him myself, and he's told me that he liked the way Waldron swung. Personally, I believe one of those Jackson boys got too gabby. But Art swears not."

"That is a story," I said gratefully. "An old outfielder who must know he's slipping recommends a busher after seeing him pop out once. And the busher jumps right in and gets his job."

I looked down the aisle toward the song birds. Art Graham, now a bench warmer, and young Waldron, whom he had touted and who was the cause of his being sent to the bench, were harmonizing at the tops of their strong and not too pleasant voices.

"And probably the strangest part of the story," I added, "is that Art doesn't seem to regret it. He and the kid appear to be the best of friends."

"Anybody who can sing is Art's friend," said Ryan.

I left him and went back to my seat to tear off my seven hundred words before we reached Springfield. I considered for a moment the advisability of asking Graham for an explanation of his wonderful bit of scouting, but decided to save that part of it for another day. I was in a hurry and, besides, Waldron was just teaching them a new "wallop," and it would have been folly for me to interrupt.

"It's on the word 'you,'" Waldron was saying. "I come down a tone; Lefty goes up a half tone, and Bill comes up two tones, Art just sings it like always. Now try her again," I heard him direct the song birds. They tried her again, making a worse noise than ever:

"I only know I love you; Love me, and the world (the world) is mine (the world is mine)."

"No," said Waldron. "Lefty missed it. If you fellas knew music, I could teach it to you with the piano when we get to Boston. On the word 'love,' in the next to the last line, we hit a regular F chord. Bill's singing the low F in the bass and Lefty's hitting middle C in the baritone, and Art's on high F and I'm up to A. Then, on the word 'you,' I come down to G, and Art hits E and Lefty goes up half a tone to C sharp, and Cole comes up from F to A in the bass. That makes a good wallop. It's a change from the F chord to the A chord. Now let's try her again," Waldron urged.

They tried her again:

"I only know I love you—"

"No, no! " said young Waldron. "Art and I were all right; but Bill came up too far, and Lefty never moved off that C. Half a tone up, Lefty. Now try her again."

We were an hour late into Springfield, and it was past six o'clock when we pulled out. I had filed my stuff, and when I came back in the car the concert was over for the time, and Art Graham was sitting alone.

"Where are your pals?" I asked.

"Gone to the diner," he replied.

"Aren't you going to eat?"

"No," he said, "I'm savin' up for the steamed clams."

I took the seat beside him.

"I sent in a story about you," I said.

"Am I fired? "he asked.

"No, nothing like that."

"Well," he said, "you must be hard up when you can't find nothin' better to write about than a old has-been."

"Cap just told me who it was that found Waldron," said I.

"Oh, that," said Art. "I don't see no story in that."

"I thought it was quite a stunt," I said. "It isn't everybody that can pick out a second Cobb by just seeing him hit a fly ball."

Graham smiled.

"No," he replied, "they's few as smart as that."

"If you ever get through playing ball," I went on, "you oughtn't to have any trouble landing a job. Good scouts don't grow on trees."

"It looks like I'm pretty near through now," said Art, still smiling. "But you won't never catch me scoutin' for nobody. It's too lonesome a job."

I had passed up lunch to retain my seat in the card game; so I was hungry. Moreover, it was evident that Graham was not going to wax garrulous on the subject of his scouting ability. I left him and sought the diner. I found a vacant chair opposite Bill Cole.

"Try the minced ham," he advised, "but lay off'n the sparrow-grass. It's tougher'n a double-header in St. Louis."

"We're over an hour late," I said.

"You'll have to do a hurry-up on your story, won't you? " asked Bill. "Or did you write it already?"

"All written and on the way."

"Well, what did you tell 'em?" he inquired. "Did you tell 'em we had a pleasant trip, and Lenke lost his shirt in the poker game, and I'm goin' to pitch to-morrow, and the Boston club's heard about it and hope it'll rain?"

"No," I said. " I gave them a regular story to-night—about how Graham picked Waldron."

"Who give it to you?"

"Ryan," I told him.

"Then you didn't get the real story," said Cole, "Ryan himself don't know the best part of it, and he ain't goin' to know it for a w'ile. He'll maybe find it out after Art's got the can, but not before. And I hope nothin' like that'll happen for twenty years. When it does happen, I want to be sent along with Art, 'cause I and him's been roomies now since 1911, and I. wouldn't hardly know how to act with him off'n the club. He's a nut all right on the singin' stuff, and if he was gone I might get a chanct to give my voice a rest. But he's a pretty good guy, even if he is crazy."

"I'd like to hear the real story," I said.

"Sure you would," he answered, "and I'd like to tell it to you. I will tell it to you if you'll give me your promise not to spill it till Art's gone. Art told it to I and Lefty in the club-house at Cleveland pretty near a nionth ago, and the three of us and Waldron is the only ones that knows it. I figure I've did pretty well to keep it to myself this long, but it seems like I got to tell somebody."

"You can depend on me," I assured him, "not to say a word about it till Art's in Minneapolis, or wherever they're going to send him."

"I guess I can trust you," said Cole. "But if von cross me, I'll shoot my fast one up there in the press coop some day and knock your teeth loose."

"Shoot," said I.

"Well," said Cole, "I s'pose Ryan told you that Art fell for the kid after just seem' him pop out."

"Yes, and Ryan said he considered it a remarkable piece of scouting."

"It was all o' that. It'd of been remarkable enough if Art'd saw the bird pop out and then recommended him. But he didn't even see him pop out."

"What are you giving me?"

"The fac's." said Bill Cole. "Art not only didn't see him pop out, but he didn't even see him with a ball suit on. He wasn't never inside the Jackson ball park in his life."

"Waldron?"

"No. Art I'm talkin' about."

"Then somebody tipped him off," I said, quickly.

"No, sir. Nobody tipped him off, neither. He went to Jackson and spent the ev'nin' at his uncle's house, and Waldron was there. Him and Art was together the whole ev'nin'. But Art didn't even ask him if he could slide feet first. And then he come back to Detroit and got Ryan to draft him. But to give you the whole story, I'll have to go back a ways. We ain't nowheres near Worcester yet, so they's no hurry, except that Art'll prob'ly be sendin' for me pretty quick to come in and learn Waldron's lost chord.

"You wasn't with this club when we had Mike McCann. But you must of heard of him; outside his pitchin', I mean. He was on the stage a couple o' winters, and he had the swellest tenor voice I ever heard. I never seen no grand opera, but I'll bet this here C'ruso or McCormack or Gadski or none o' them had nothin' on him for a pure tenor. Every note as clear as a bell. You couldn't hardly keep your eyes dry when he'd tear off 'Silver Threads' or 'The River Shannon.'

"Well, when Art was still with the Washin'ton club yet, I and Lefty and Mike used to pal round together and onct or twict we'd hit up some harmony. I couldn't support a fam'ly o' Mormons with my voice, but it was better in them days than it is now. I used to carry the lead, and Lefty'd hit the baritone and Mike the tenor. We didn't have no bass. But most o' the time we let Mike do the singin' alone, 'cause he had us outclassed, and the other boys kept tellin' us to shut up and give 'em a treat. First it'd be ' Silver Threads' and then 'Jerusalem' and then 'My Wild Irish Rose' and this and that, whatever the boys ast him for. Jake Martin used to say he couldn't help a short pair if Mike wasn't singin'.

"Finally Ryan pulled off the trade with Griffith, and Graham come on our club. Then they wasn't no more solo work. They made a bass out o' me, and Art sung the lead, and Mike and Lefty took care o' the tenor and baritone. Art didn't care what the other boys wanted to hear. They could holler their heads off for Mike to sing a solo, but no sooner'd Mike start singin' than Art'd chime in with him and pretty soon we'd all four be goin' it. Art's a nut on singin', but he don't care nothin' about list'nin', not even to a canary. He'd rather harmonize than hit one past the outfielders with two on.

"At first we done all our serenadin' on the train. Art'd get us out o' bed early so's we could be through breakfast and back in the ear in time to tear off a few before we got to wherever we was goin'.

"It got so's Art wouldn't leave us alone in the different towns 'we played at. We couldn't go to no show or nothin'. We had to stick in the hotel and sing, up in our room or Mike's. And then he went so nuts over it that he got Mike to come and room in the same house with him at home, and I and Lefty was supposed to help keep the neighbors awake every night. O' course we had mornin' practice w'ile we was home, and Art used to have us come to the park early and get in a little harmony before we went on the field. But Ryan finally nailed that. He says that when he ordered mornin' practice he meant baseball and not no minstrel show.

"Then Lefty, who wasn't married, goes and gets himself a girl. I met her a couple o' times, and she looked all right. Lefty might of married her if Art'd of left him alone. But nothin' doin'. We was home all through June onct, and instead o' comin' round nights to sing with us, Lefty'd take this here doll to one o' the parks or somewheres. Well, sir, Art was pretty near wild. He scouted round till he'd found out why Lefty'd quit us and then he tried pretty near everybody else on the club to see if they wasn't some one who could hit the baritone. They wasn't nobody. So the next time we went on the road, Art give Lefty a earful about what a sucker a man was to get married, and looks wasn't everything and the girl was prob'ly after Lefty's money and he wasn't hem' a good fella to break up the quartette and spoil our good times, and so on, and kept pesterin' and teasin' Lefty till he give the girl up. I'd of saw Art in the Texas League before I'd of shook a girl to please him, but you know these left-handers.

"Art had it all framed that we was goin' on the stage, the four of us, and he seen a vaudeville man in New York and got us booked for eight hundred a week—I don't know if it was one week or two. But he sprung it on me in September and says we could get solid bookin' from October to March; so I ast him what he thought my Missus would say when I told her I couldn't get enough o' hem' away from home from March to October, so I was figurin' on travelin' the vaudeville circuit the other four or five months and makin' it unanimous? Art says I was tied to a woman's apron and all that stuff, but I give him the cold stare and he had to pass up that dandy little scheme.

"At that, I guess we could of got by on the stage all right. Mike was better than this here Waldron and I hadn't wore my voice out yet on the coachin' line, tellin' the boys to touch all the bases.

"They was about five or six songs that we could kill. 'Adeline' was our star piece. Remember where it comes in, 'Your fair face beams'? Mike used to go away up on 'fair.' Then they was 'The Old Millstream' and 'Put on Your Old Gray Bonnet.' I done some fancy work in that one. Then they was 'Down in Jungle Town' that we had pretty good. And then they was one that maybe you never heard. I don't know the name of it. It run somethin' like this."

Bill sottoed his voice so that I alone could hear the beautiful refrain:

"'Years, years, I've waited years Only to see you, just to call you 'dear.' Come, come, I love but thee, Come to your sweetheart's arms; come back to me.'

"That one had a lot o' wallops in it, and we didn't overlook none o' them. The boys used to make us sing it six or seven times a night. But 'Down in the Cornfield' was Art's favor-ight. They was a part in that where I sung the lead down low and the other three done a banjo stunt. Then they was 'Castle on the Nile' and 'Come Back to Erin' and a whole lot more.

"Well, the four of us wasn't hardly ever separated for three years. We was practisin' all the w'ile like as if we was goin' to play the big time, and we never made a nickel off'n it. The only audience we had was the ball players or the people travelin' on the same trains or stoppin' at the same hotels, and they got it all for nothin'. But we had a good time, 'specially Art.

"You know what a pitcher Mike was. He could go in there stone cold and stick ten out o' twelve over that old plate with somethin' on 'em. And he was the willin'est guy in the world. He pitched his own game every third or fourth day, and between them games he was warmin' up all the time to go in for somebody else. In 1911, when we was up in the race for aw'ile, he pitched eight games out o' twenty, along in September, and win seven o' them, and besides that, he finished up five o' the twelve he didn't start. We didn't win the pennant, and I've always figured that them three weeks killed Mike.

"Anyway, he wasn't worth nothin' to the club the next year; but they carried him along, hopin' he'd come back and show somethin'. But he was pretty near through, and he knowed it. I knowed it, too, and so did everybody else on the club, only Graham. Art never got wise till the trainin' trip two years ago this last spring. Then he come to me one day.

"'Bill,' he says, 'I don't believe Mike's comin' back.'

"'Well,' I says, 'you're gettin' so's they can't nobody hide nothin' from you. Next thing you'll be findin' out that Sam Crawford can hit.'

"'Never mind the comical stuff,' he says. 'They ain't no joke about this!'

"'No,' I says, 'and I never said they was. They'll look a long w'ile before they find another pitcher like Mike.'

"'Pitcher my foot!' says Art. 'I don't care if they have to pitch the bat boy. But when Mike goes, where'll our quartette be?'

"'Well,' I says, 'do you get paid every first and fifteenth for singin' or for crownin' that old pill?'

"'If you couldn't talk about money, you'd be deaf and dumb,' says Art.

"'But you ain't playin' ball because it's fun, are you?'

"'No,' he says, 'they ain't no fun for me in playin' ball. They's no fun doin' nothin' but harmonizin', and if Mike goes, I won't even have that.'

"'I and you and Lefty can harmonize,' I says.

"'It'd be swell stuff harmonizin' without no tenor,' says Art. 'It'd be like swingin' without no bat.'

"Well, he ast me did I think the club'd carry Mike through another season, and I told him they'd already carried him a year without him hem' no good to them, and I figured if he didn't show somethin' his first time out, they'd ask for waivers. Art kept broodin' and broodin' about it till they wasn't hardly no livin' with him. If he ast me onet he ast me a thousand tmmes if

I didn't think they might maybe hold onto Mike another season on account of all he'd did for 'em. I kept tellin' him I didn't think so; but that didn't satisfy him and he finally went to Ryan and ast him point blank.

"'Are you goin' to keep McCann? 'Art ast him.

"'If he's goin' to do us any good, I am,' says Ryan. "If he ain't, he'll have to look for another job.'

"After that, all through the trainin' trip, he was right on Mike's heels.

"'How does the old souper feel?' he'd ask him.

"'Great!' Mike'd say.

"Then Art'd watch him warm up, to see if he had anything on the ball.

"'He's comin' fine,' he'd tell me. 'His curve broke to-day just as good as I ever seen it.'

"But that didn't fool me, or it didn't fool Mike neither. He could throw about four hooks and then he was through. And he could of hit you in the head with his fast one and you'd of thought you had a rash.

"One night, just before the season opened up, we was singin' on the train, and when we got through, Mike says:

"'Well, boys, you better be lookin' for another C'ruso.'

"'What are you talkin' about?' says Art.

"'I'm talkin' about myself,' says Mike. 'I'll be up there in Minneapolis this summer, pitchin' onct a week and swappin' stories about the Civil War with Joe Cantillon.'

"'You're crazy,' says Art. 'Your arm's as good as I ever seen it.'

"'Then,' says Mike, 'you must of been playin' blindfolded all these years. This is just between us, 'cause Ryan'll find it out for himself; my arm's rotten, and I can't do nothin' to help it.'

"Then Art got sore as a boil.

"'You're a yellow, quittin' dog,' he says. 'Just because you conic round a little slow, you talk about Minneapolis. Why don't you resign off'n. the club?'

"'I might just as well,' Mike says, and left us.

"You'd of thought that Art would of gave up then, 'cause when a ball player admits he's slippin', you can bet your last nickel that he's through. Most o' them stalls along and tries to kid themselves and everybody else long after they know they're gone. But Art kept talkin' like they was still some hope o' Mike comin' round, and when Ryan told us one night in St. Louis that he was goin' to give Mike his chanct, the next day, Art was as nervous as a bride goin' to get married. I wasn't nervous. I just felt sorry, 'cause I knowed the old boy was hopeless.

"Ryan had told him he was goin' to work if the weather suited him. Well, the day was perfect. So Mike went out to the park along about noon and took Jake with him to warm up. Jake told me afterwards that

Mike was throwin', just easy like, from half-past twelve till the rest of us got there. He was tryin' to heat up the old souper and he couldn't of ast for a better break in the weather, but they wasn't enough sunshine in the world to make that old whip crack.

"Well, sir, you'd of thought to see Art that Mike was his son or his brother or somebody and just breakin' into the league. Art wasn't in the outfield practisin' more than two minutes. He come in and stood behind Mike w'ile he was warmin' up and kept tellin' how good he looked, hut the only guy he was kiddin' was himself.

"Then the game starts and our club goes in and gets three runs.

"'Pretty soft for you now, Mike,' says Art, on the bench. 'They can't score three off'n you in three years.'

"Say, it's lucky he ever got the side out in the first innin'. Everybody that come up hit one on the pick, but our infield pulled two o' the greatest plays I ever seen and they didn't score. In the second, we got three more, and I thought maybe the old bird was goin' to be lucky enough to scrape through.

"For four or five innin's, he got the grandest support that was ever gave a pitcher; but I'll swear that what he throwed up there didn't have no more on it than September Morning. Every time Art come to the bench, he says to Mike, 'Keep it up, old boy. You got more than you ever had.'

"Well, in the seventh, Mike still had 'em shut out, and we was six runs to the good. Then a couple o' the St. Louis boys hit 'em where they couldn't nobody reach 'em and they was two on and two out. Then somebody got a hold o' one and sent it on a line to the left o' second base. I forgot who it was now; but whoever it was, he was supposed to be a right field hitter, and Art was layin' over the other way for him. Art started with the crack o' the bat, and I never seen a man make a better try for a ball. He had it judged perfect; but Cobb or Speaker or none o' them couldn't of catched it. Art just managed to touch it by stretchin' to the limit. It went on to the fence and everybody come in. They didn't score no more in that innin'.

"Then Art come in from the field and what do you think he tried to pull?

"'I don't know what was the matter with me on that fly ball,' he says. 'I ought to caught it in my pants pocket. But I didn't get started till it was right on top o' me.'

"'You misjudged it, didn't you?' says Ryan.

"'I certainly did,' says Art without crackin'.

"'Well,' says Ryan, 'I wisht you'd misjudge all o' them that way. I never seen a better play on a ball.'

"So then Art knowed they wasn't no more use trying to alibi the old boy.

"Mike had a turn at bat and when he come back, Ryan ast him how he felt.

"'I guess I can get six more o' them out,' he says.

"Well, they didn't score in the eighth, and when the ninth come Ryan sent I and Lefty out to warm up. We throwed a few w'ile our club was battin'; but when it come St. Louis' last chanct, we was too much interested in the ball game to know if we was throwin' or bakin' biscuits.

"The first guy hits a line drive, and somebody jumps a mile in the air and stabs it. The next fella fouled out, and they was only one more to get. And then what do you think come off? Whoever it was hittin' lifted a fly ball to centre field. Art didn't have to move out of his tracks. I've saw him catch a hundred just like it behind his back. But you know what he was thinkin'. He was sayin' to himself, 'If I nail this one, we're li'ble to keep our tenor singer a w'ile longer.' And he dropped it.

"Then they was five base hits that sounded like the fourth o' July, and they come so fast that Ryan didn't have time to send for I or Lefty. Anyway, I guess he thought he might as well leave Mike in there and take it.

"They wasn't no singin' in the clubhouse after that game. I and Lefty always let the others start it. Mike, o' course, didn't feel like no jubilee, and Art was so busy tryin' not to let nobody see him cry that he kept his head clear down in his socks. Finally he beat it for town all alone, and we didn't see nothin' of him till after supper. Then he got us together and we all went up to Mike's room.

"'I want to try this here " Old Girl o' Mine,"' he says.

"'Better sing our old stuff,' says Mike. 'This looks like the last time.'

"Then Art choked up and it was ten minutes before he could get goin'. We sung everything we knowed, and it was two o'clock in the mornin' before Art had enough. Ryan come in after midnight and set a w'ile listenin', but he didn't chase us to bed. He knowed better'n any of us that it was a farewell. When I and Art was startin' for our room, Art turned to Mike and says:

"'Old boy, I'd of gave every nickel I ever owned to of caught that fly ball.'

"'I know you would,' Mike says, 'and I know what made you drop it. But don't worry about it, 'cause it was just a question o' time, and if I'd of got away with that game, they'd of murdered some o' the infielders next time I started.'

"Mike was sent home the next day, and we didn't see him again. He was shipped to Minneapolis before we got back. And the rest o' the season I might as well of lived in a cemetery w'ile we was on the road. Art was so bad that I thought onct or twict I'd have to change roommies. Onct in a w'ile he'd start hummin' and then he'd break off short and growl at me. He tried out two or three o' the other boys on the club to see if he couldn't find a new tenor singer, but nothin' doin'. One night he made Lefty try the tenor. Well,

Lefty's voice is bad enough down low. When he gets up about so high, you think you're in the stockyards.

"And Art had a rotten year in baseball, too. The old boy's still pretty near as good on a fly ball as anybody in the league; but you ought to saw him before his legs begin to give out. He could cover as much ground as Speaker and he was just as sure. But the year Mike left us, he missed pretty near half as many as he got. He told me one night, he says:

"'Do you know, Bill, I stand out there and pray that nobody'll hit one to me. Every time I see one comin' I think o' that one I dropped for Mike in St. Louis, and then I'm just as li'ble to have it come down on my bean as in my glove.'

"'You're crazy,' I says, 'to let a thing like that make a bum out o' you.'

"But he kept on droppin' fly balls till Ryan was talkin' about settin' him on the bench where it wouldn't hurt nothin' if his nerve give out. But Ryan didn't have nobody else to play out there, so Art held on.

"He come back the next spring—-that's a year ago—feelin' more cheerful and like himself than I'd saw him for a long w'ile. And they was a kid named Burton tryin' out for second base that could sing pretty near as good as Mike. It didn't take Art more'n a day to find this out, and every mornin' and night for a few days the four of us would be together, hittin' her up. But the kid didn't have no more idea o' how to play the bag than Charley Chaplin. Art seen in a minute that he couldn't never beat Cragin out of his job, so what does he do but take him out and try and learn him to play the outfield. He wasn't no worse there than at second base; he couldn't of been. But before he'd practised out there three days they was bruises all over his head and shoulders where fly balls had hit him. Well, the kid wasn't with us long enough to see the first exhibition game, and after he'd went, Art was Old Man Grump again.

"'What's the matter with you?' I says to him. 'You was all smiles the day we reported and now you could easy pass for a undertaker.'

"'Well,' he says, 'I had a great winter, singin' all the w'ile. We got a good quartette down home and I never enjoyed myself as much in my life. And I kind o' had a hunch that I was goin' to be lucky and find somebody amongst the bushers that could hit up the old tenor.'

"'Your hunch was right,' I says. 'That Burton kid was as good a tenor as you'd want.'

"'Yes,' he says, 'and my hunch could of played ball just as good as him.'

"Well, sir, if you didn't never room with a corpse, you don't know what a whale of a time I had all last season. About the middle of August he was at his worst.

"'Bill,' he says, 'I'm goin' to leave this old baseball flat on its back if somethin' don't happen. I can't stand these here lonesome nights. I ain't like the rest o' the boys that can go and set all ev'nin' at a pitcher show or hang round them Dutch gardens. I got to be singin' or I am mis'rable.'

"'Go ahead and sing,' says I. 'I'll try and keep the cops back.'

"'No,' he says, 'I don't want to sing alone. I want to harmonize and we can't do that 'cause we ain't got no tenor.'

"I don't know if you'll believe me or not, but sure as we're settin' here he went to Ryan one day in Philly and tried to get him to make a trade for Harper.

"'What do I want him for?' says Ryan.

"'I hear he ain't satisfied,' says Art.

"'I ain't runnin' no ball players' benefit association,' says Ryan, and Art had to give it up. But he didn't want Harper on the club for no other reason than because he's a tenor singer!

"And then come that Dee-troit trip, and Art got permission to go to Jackson. He says he intended to drop in at the ball park, but his uncle wanted to borry some money off'n him on a farm, so Art had to drive out and see the farm. Then, that night, this here Waldron was up to call on Art's cousin—a swell doll, Art tells me. And Waldron set down to the py-ana and begin to sing and play. Then it was all off; they wasn't no spoonin' in the parlor that night. Art wouldn't leave the kid get off'n the py-ana stool long enough to even find out if the girl was a blonde or a brunette.

"O' course Art knowed the boy was with the Jackson club as soon as they was interduced, 'cause Art's uncle says somethin' about the both o' them hem' ball players, and so on. But Art swears he never thought o' recommendin' him till the kid got up to go home. Then he ast him what position did he play and found out all about him, only o' course Waldron didn't tell him how good he was 'cause he didn't know himself.

"So Art ast him would he like a trial in the big show, and the kid says he would. Then Art says maybe the kid would hear from him, and then Waldron left and Art went to bed, and he says he stayed awake all night plannin' the thing out and wonderin' would he have the nerve to pull it off. You see he thought that if Ryan fell for it, Waldron'd join us as soon as his season was over and then Ryan'd see he wasn't no good; but he'd prob'ly keep him till we was through for the year, and Art could alibi himself some way, say he'd got the wrong name or somethin'. All he wanted, he says was to have the kid along the last month or six weeks, so's we could harmonize. A nut? I guess not.

"Well, as you know, Waldron got sick and didn't report, and when Art seen him on the train this spring he couldn't hardly believe his eyes. He thought surely the kid would of been canned durin' the winter without no trial.

"Here's another hot one. When we went out the first day for practice, Art takes the kid off in a corner and tries to learn him enough baseball so's he won't show himself up and get sent away somewheres before we had a little benefit from his singin'. Can you imagine that? Tryin' to learn this kid baseball, when he was born with a slidin' pad on.

"You know the rest of it. They wasn't never no question about Waldron makin' good. It's just like everybody says—he's the best natural ball player that's broke in since Cobb. They ain't nothin' he can't do. But it is a funny thing that Art's job should be the one he'd get . I spoke about that to Art when he give me the story.

"'Well,' he says, 'I can't expect everything to break right. I figure I'm lucky to of picked a guy that's good enough to hang on. I'm in stronger with Ryan right now, and with the old man, too, than when I was out there playin' every day. Besides, the bench is a pretty good place to watch the game from. And this club won't be shy a tenor singer for nine years.'

"'No,' I says, 'but they'll be shy a lead and a baritone and a bass before I and you and Lefty is much older.'

"'What of it?' he says. 'We'll look up old Mike and all go somewheres and live together.'"

We were nearing Worcester. Bill Cole and I arose from our table and started back toward our car. In the first vestibule we encountered Buck, the trainer.

"Mr. Graham's been lookin' all over for you, Mr. Cole," he said.

"I've been rehearsin' my part," said Bill.

We found Art Graham, Lefty, and young Waldron in Art's seat. The kid was talking.

"Lefty missed it again. If you fellas knew music, I could teach it to you on the piano when we get to Boston. Lefty, on the word 'love,' in the next to the last line, you're on middle C. Then, on the word 'you,' you slide up half a tone. That'd ought to be a snap, but you don't get it. I'm on high A and come down to G and Bill's on low F and comes up to A. Art just sings the regular two notes, F and B. It's a change from the F chord to the A chord. It makes a dandy wallop and it ought to be a —"

"Here's Bill now," interrupted Lefty, as he caught sight of Cole.

Art Graham treated his roommate to a cold stare. "Where the h—l have you been?" he said angrily.

"Lookin' for the lost chord," said Bill.

"Set down here and learn this," growled Art. "We won't never get it if we don't work."

"Yes, let's tackle her again," said Waldron. "Bill comes up two full tones, from F to A. Lefty goes up half a tone, Art sings just like always, and I come down a tone. Now try her again."

Two years ago it was that Bill Cole told me that story. Two weeks ago Art Graham boarded the evening train on one of the many roads that lead to Minneapolis.

The day Art was let out, I cornered Ryan in the club-house after the others had dressed and gone home.

"Did you ever know," I asked, "that Art recommended Waldron without having seen him in a ball suit?"

"I told you long ago how Art picked Waldron," he said.

"Yes," said I, "but you didn't have the right story." So I gave it to him.

"You newspaper fellas," he said when I had done, "are the biggest suckers in the world. Now I've never given you a bad steer in my life. But you don't believe what I tell you and you go and fall for one of Bill Cole's hop dreams. Don't you know that he was the biggest liar in baseball? He'd tell you that Walter Johnson was Jack's father if he thought he could get away with it. And that bunk he gave you about Waldron. Does it sound reasonable?

"Just as reasonable," I replied, "as the stuff about Art's grabbing him after seeing him pop out."

"I don't claim he did," said Ryan. "That's what Art told me. One of those Jackson ball players could give you the real truth, only of course he wouldn't, because if Hodges ever found it out he'd shoot him full of holes. Art Graham's no fool. He isn't touting ball players because they can sing tenor or alto or anything else."

Nevertheless, I believe Bill Cole; else I wouldn't print the story. And Ryan would believe, too, if he weren't in such a mood these days that he disagrees with everybody. For in spite of Waldron's wonderful work, and he is at his best right now, the club hasn't done nearly as well as when Art and Bill and Lefty were still with us.

There seems to be a lack of harmony.

Alibi Ike

I

His right name was Frank X. Farrell, and I guess the X stood for "Excuse me." Because he never pulled a play, good or bad, on or off the field, without apologizin' for it.

"Alibi Ike" was the name Carey wished on him the first day he reported down South. O' course we all cut out the "Alibi" part of it right away for the fear he would overhear it and bust somebody. But we called him "Ike" right to his face and the rest of it was understood by everybody on the club except Ike himself.

He ast me one time, he says:

"What do you all call me Ike for? I ain't no Yid."

"Carey give you the name," I says. "It's his nickname for everybody he takes a likin' to."

"He mustn't have only a few friends then," says Ike. "I never heard him say 'Ike' to nobody else."

But I was goin' to tell you about Carey namin' him. We'd been workin' out two weeks and the pitchers was showin' somethin' when this bird joined us. His first day out he stood up there so good and took such a reef at the old pill that he had everyone lookin'. Then him and Carey was together in left field, catchin' fungoes, and it was after we was through for the day that Carey told me about him.

"What do you think of Alibi Ike?" ast Carey.

"Who's that? " I says.

"This here Farrell in the outfield," says Carey.

"He looks like he could hit," I says.

"Yes," says Carey, "but he can't hit near as good as he can apologize."

Then Carey went on to tell me what Ike had been pullin' out there. He'd dropped the first fly ball that was hit to him and told Carey his glove wasn't broke in good yet, and Carey says the glove could easy of been Kid Gleason's gran'father. He made a whale of a catch out o' the next one and Carey says "Nice work!" or somethin' like that, but Ike says he could of caught the ball with his back turned only he slipped when he started after it and, besides that, the air currents fooled him.

"I thought you done well to get to the ball," says Carey.

"I ought to been settin' under it," says Ike.

"What did you hit last year?" Carey ast him.

"I had malaria most o' the season," says Ike. "I wound up with .356."

"Where would I have to go to get malaria?" says Carey, but Ike didn't wise up.

I and Carey and him set at the same table together for supper. It took him half an hour longer'n us to eat because he had to excuse himself every time he lifted his fork.

"Doctor told me I needed starch," he'd say, and then toss a shoveful o' potatoes into him. Or, "They ain't much meat on one o' these chops," he'd tell us, and grab another one. Or he'd say: "Nothin' like onions for a cold," and then he'd dip into the perfumery.

"Better try that apple sauce," says Carey. "It'll help your malaria."

"Whose malaria?" says Ike. He'd forgot already why he didn't only hit .356 last year.

I and Carey begin to lead him on.

"Whereabouts did you say your home was?" I ast him. "I live with my folks," he says. "We live in Kansas City—not right down in the business part—outside a ways."

"How's that come?" says Carey. "I should think you'd get rooms in the post office."

But Ike was too busy curin' his cold to get that one.

"Are you married?" I ast him.

"No," he says. "I never run round much with girls, except to shows onct in a wile and parties and dances and roller skatin'."

"Never take 'em to the prize fights, eh?" says Carey.

"We don't have no real good bouts," says Ike. "Just bush stuff. And I never figured a boxin' match was a place for the ladies."

Well, after supper he pulled a cigar out and lit it. I was just goin' to ask him what he done it for, but he beat me to it.

"Kind o' rests a man to smoke after a good workout," he says. "Kind o' settles a man's supper, too."

"Looks like a pretty good cigar," says Carey.

"Yes," says Ike. "A friend o' mine give it to me—a fella in Kansas City that runs a billiard room."

"Do you play billiards?" I ast him.

"I used to play a fair game," he says. "I'm all out o' practice now—can't hardly make a shot."

We coaxed him into a four-handed battle, him and Carey against Jack Mack and I. Say, he couldn't play billiards as good as Willie Hoppe; not quite. But to hear him tell it, he didn't make a good shot all evenin'. I'd leave him an awful-lookin' layout and he'd gather 'em up in one try and then run a couple o' hundred, and between every carom he'd say he'd put too much stuff on the ball, or the English didn't take, or the table wasn't true, or his stick was crooked, or somethin'. And all the time he had the balls actin' like they was Dutch soldiers and him Kaiser William. We started out to play fifty points, but we had to make it a thousand so as I and Jack and Carey could try the table.

The four of us set round the lobby a wile after we was through playin', and when it got along toward bedtime Carey whispered to me and says:

"Ike'd like to go to bed, but he can't think up no excuse."

Carey hadn't hardly finished whisperin' when Ike got up and pulled it:

"Well, good night, boys," he says. "I ain't sleepy, but I got some gravel in my shoes and it's killin' my feet."

We knowed he hadn't never left the hotel since we'd came in from the grounds and changed our clo'es. So Carey says:

"I should think they'd take them gravel pits out o' the billiard room."

But Ike was already on his way to the elevator, limpin'.

"He's got the world beat," says Carey to Jack and I. "I've knew lots o' guys that had an alibi for every mistake they made; I've heard pitchers say that the ball slipped when somebody cracked one off'n 'em; I've heard infielders complain of a sore arm after heavin' one into the stand, and I've saw outfielders tooken sick with a dizzy spell when they've misjudged a fly ball. But this baby can't even go to bed without apologizin', and I bet he excuses himself to the razor when he gets ready to shave."

"And at that," says Jack, "he's goin' to make us a good man."

"Yes," says Carey, "unless rheumatism keeps his battin' average down to .400."

Well, sir, Ike kept whalin' away at the ball all through the trip till everybody knowed he'd won a job. Cap had him in there regular the last few exhibition games and told the newspaper boys a week before the season opened that he was goin' to start him in Kane's place.

"You're there, kid," says Carey to Ike, the night Cap made the 'nnouncement. "They ain't many boys that wins a big league berth their third year out."

"I'd of been up here a year ago," says Ike, "only I was bent over all season with lumbago."

II

It rained down in Cincinnati one day and somebody organized a little game o' cards. They was shy two men to make six and ast I and Carey to play.

"I'm with you if you get Ike and make it seven-handed," says Carey.

So they got a hold of Ike and we went up to Smitty's room.

"I pretty near forgot how many you deal," says Ike. "It's been a long wile since I played."

I and Carey give each other the wink, and sure enough, he was just as ig'orant about poker as billiards. About the second hand, the pot was opened two or three ahead of him, and they was three in when it come his turn. It cost a buck, and he throwed in two.

"It's raised, boys," somebody says.

"Gosh, that's right, I did raise it," says Ike.

"Takeout a buck if you didn't mean to tilt her," says Carey.

"No," says Ike, "I'll leave it go."

Well, it was raised back at him and then he made another mistake and raised again. They was only three left in when the draw come. Smitty'd opened with a pair o' kings and he didn't help 'em. Ike stood pat. The guy that'd raised him back was flushin' and he didn't fill. So Smitty checked and Ike bet and didn't get no call. He tossed his hand away, but I grabbed it and give it a look. He had king, queen, jack and two tens. Alibi Ike he must have seen me peekin', for he leaned over and whispered to me.

"I overlooked my hand," he says. "I thought all the wile it was a straight."

"Yes," I says, "that's why you raised twice by mistake."

They was another pot that he come into with tens and fours. It was tilted a couple o' times and two o' the strong fellas drawed ahead of Ike. They each drawed one. So Ike throwed away his little pair and come out with four tens. And they was four treys against him. Carey'd looked at Ike's discards and then he says:

"This lucky bum busted two pair."

"No, no, I didn't," says Ike.

"Yes, yes, you did," says Carey, and showed us the two fours. "What do you know about that? " says Ike. "I'd of swore one was a five spot."

Well, we hadn't had no pay day yet, and after a wile everybody except Ike was goin' shy. I could see him gettin' restless and I was wonderin' how he'd make the get-away. He tried two or three times. "I got to buy some collars before supper," he says.

"No hurry," says Smitty. "The stores here keeps open all night in April."

After a minute he opened up again.

"My uncle out in Nebraska ain't expected to live," he says. "I ought to send a telegram."

"Would that save him?" says Carey.

"No, it sure wouldn't," says Ike, "but I ought to leave my old man know where I'm at."

"When did you hear about your uncle?" says Carey.

"Just this mornin'," says Ike.

"Who told you? "ast Carey.

"I got a wire from my old man," says Ike.

"Well," says Carey, "your old man knows you're still here yet this afternoon if you was here this mornin'. Trains leavin' Cincinnati in the middle o' the day don't carry no ball clubs."

"Yes," says Ike, "that's true. But he don't know where I'm goin' to be next week."

"Ain't he got no schedule?" ast Carey.

"I sent him one openin' day," says Ike, "but it takes mail a long time to get to Idaho."

"I thought your old man lived in Kansas City," says Carey.

"He does when he's home," says Ike.

"But now," says Carey, "I s'pose he's went to Idaho so as he can be near your sick uncle in Nebraska."

"He's visitin' my other uncle in Idaho."

"Then how does he keep posted about your sick uncle?" ast Carey.

"He don't," says Ike. "He don't even know my other uncle's sick. That's why I ought to wire and tell him."

"Good night!" says Carey.

"What town in Idaho is your old man at?" I says.

Ike thought it over.

"No town at all," he says. "But he's near a town."

"Near what town?" I says.

"Yuma," says Ike.

Well, by this time he'd lost two or three pots and he was desperate. We was playin' just as fast as we could, because we seen we couldn't hold him much longer. But he was tryin' so hard to frame an escape that he couldn't pay no attention to the cards, and it looked like we'd get his whole pile away from him if we could make him stick.

The telephone saved him. The minute it begun to ring, five of us jumped for it. But Ike was there first.

"Yes," he says, answerin' it. "This is him. I'll come right down."

And he slammed up the receiver and beat it out o' the door without even sayin' good-by.

"Smitty'd ought to locked the door," says Carey.

"What did he win?" ast Carey.

We figured it up—sixty-odd bucks.

"And the next time we ask him to play," says Carey, "his fingers will be so stiff he can't hold the cards."

Well, we set round a wile talkin' it over, and pretty soon the telephone rung again. Smitty answered it. It was a friend of his'n from Hamilton and he wanted to know why Smitty didn't hurry down. He was the one that had called before and Ike had told him he was Smitty.

"Ike'd ought to split with Smitty's friend," says Carey.

"No," I says, "he'll need all he won. It costs money to buy collars and to send telegrams from Cincinnati to your old man in Texas and keep him posted on the health o' your uncle in Cedar Rapids, D. C."

III

And you ought to heard him out there on that field! They wasn't a day when he didn't pull six or seven, and it didn't make no difference whether he was goin' good or bad. If he popped up in the pinch he should of made a base hit and the reason he didn't was so-and-so. And if he cracked one for three bases he ought to had a home run, only the ball wasn't lively, or the wind brought it back, or he tripped on a lump o' dirt, roundin' first base.

They was one afternoon in New York when he beat all records. Big Marquard was workin' against us and he was good.

In the first innin' Ike hit one clear over that right field stand, but it was a few feet foul. Then he got another foul and then the count come to two and two. Then Rube slipped one acrost on him and he was called out.

"What do you know about that!" he says afterward on the bench. "I lost count. I thought it was three and one, and I took a strike."

"You took a strike all right," says Carey. "Even the umps knowed it was a strike."

"Yes," says Ike, "but you can bet I wouldn't of took it if I'd knew it was the third one. The score board had it wrong."

"That score board ain't for you to look at," says Cap. "It's for you to hit that old pill against."

"Well," says Ike, "I could of hit that one over the score board if I'd knew it was the third."

"Was it a good ball? " I says.

"Well, no, it wasn't," says Ike. "It was inside."

"How far inside?" says Carey.

"Oh, two or three inches or half a foot," says Ike.

"I guess you wouldn't of threatened the score board with it then," says Cap.

"I'd of pulled it down the right foul line if I hadn't thought he'd call it a ball," says Ike.

Well, in New York's part o' the innin' Doyle cracked one and Ike run back a mile and a half and caught it with one hand. We was all sayin' what a whale of a play it was, but he had to apologize just the same as for gettin' struck out.

"That stand's so high," he says, "that a man don't never see a ball till it's right on top o' you."

"Didn't you see that one? "ast Cap.

"Not at first," says Ike; "not till it raised up above the roof o' the stand."

"Then why did you start back as soon as the ball was hit?" says Cap.

"I knowed by the sound that he'd got a good hold of it," says Ike.

"Yes," says Cap, "but how'd you know what direction to run in?"

"Doyle usually hits 'em that way, the way I run," says Ike.

"Why don't you play blindfolded?" says Carey.

"Might as well, with that big high stand to bother a man," says Ike. "If I could of saw the ball all the time I'd of got it in my hip pocket."

Along in the fifth we was one run to the bad and Ike got on with one out. On the first ball throwed to Smitty, Ike went down. The ball was outside and Meyers throwed Ike out by ten feet.

You could see Ike's lips movin' all the way to the bench and when he got there he had his piece learned.

"Why didn't he swing?" he says.

"Why didn't you wait for his sign?" says Cap.

"He give me his sign," says Ike.

"What is his sign with you?" says Cap.

"Pickin' up some dirt with his right hand," says Ike.

"Well, I didn't see him do it," Cap says.

"He done it all right," says Ike.

Well, Smitty went out and they wasn't no more argument till they come in for the next innin'. Then Cap opened it up.

"You fellas better get your signs straight," he says.

"Do you mean me? " says Smitty.

"Yes," Cap says. "What's your sign with Ike?"

"Slidin' my left hand up to the end o' the bat and back," says Smitty.

"Do you hear that, Ike?" ast Cap.

"What of it?" says Ike.

"You says his sign was pickin' up dirt and he says it's slidin' his hand. Which is right?"

"I'm right," says Smitty. "But if you're arguin' about him goin' last innin', I didn't give him no sign."

"You pulled your cap down with your right hand, didn't you? " ast Ike.

"Well, s'pose I did," says Smitty. "That don't mean nothin'. I never told you to take that for a sign, did I?"

"I thought maybe you meant to tell me and forgot," says Ike. They couldn't none of us answer that and they wouldn't of been no more said if Ike had of shut up. But wile we was settin' there Carey got on with two out and stole second clean.

"There!" says Ike. "That's what I was tryin' to do and I'd of got away with it if Smitty'd swang and bothered the Indian."

"Oh!" says Smitty. "You was tryin' to steal then, was you? I thought you claimed I give you the hit and run."

"I didn't claim no such a thing," says Ike. "I thought maybe you might of gave me a sign, but I was goin' anyway because I thought I had a good start."

Cap prob'ly would of hit him with a bat, only just about that time Doyle booted one on Hayes and Carey come acrost with the run that tied.

Well, we go into the ninth finally, one and one, and Marquard walks McDonald with nobody out.

"Lay it down," says Cap to Ike.

And Ike goes up there with orders to bunt and cracks the first ball into that right-field stand! It was fair this time, and we're two ahead, but I didn't think about that at the time. I was too busy watchin' Cap's face. First he turned pale and then he got red as fire and then he got blue and purple, and finally he just laid back and busted out laughin'. So we wasn't afraid to laugh ourselfs when we seen him doin' it, and when Ike come in everybody on the bench was in hysterics.

But instead o' takin' advantage, Ike had to try and excuse himself. His play was to shut up and he didn't know how to make it.

"Well," he says, "if I hadn't hit quite so quick at that one I bet it'd of cleared the center-field fence."

Cap stopped laughin'.

"It'll cost you plain fifty," he says.

"What for? " says Ike.

"When I say 'bunt' I mean 'bunt,'" says Cap.

"You didn't say 'bunt,'" says Ike.

"I says 'Lay it down,'" says Cap. "If that don't mean 'bunt,' what does it mean?"

"'Lay it down' means 'bunt' all right," says Ike, "but I understood you to say 'Lay on it.'"

"All right," says Cap, "and the little misunderstandin' will cost you fifty."

Ike didn't say nothin' for a few minutes. Then he had another bright idear.

"I was just kiddin' about misunderstandin' you," he says. "I knowed you wanted me to bunt."

"Well, then, why didn't you bunt?" ast Cap.

"I was goin' to on the next ball," says Ike. "But I thought if I took a good wallop I'd have 'em all fooled. So I walloped at the first one to fool 'em, and I didn't have no intention o' hittin' it."

"You tried to miss it, did you?" says Cap.

"Yes," says Ike.

"How'd you happen to hit it?" ast Cap.

"Well," Ike says, "I was lookin' for him to throw me a fast one and I was goin' to awing under it. But he come with a hook and I met it right square where I was swingin' to go under the fast one."

"Great!" says Cap. "Boys," he says, "Ike's learned how to hit Marquard's curve. Pretend a fast one's comin' and then try to miss it. It's a good thing to know and Ike'd ought to be willin' to pay for the lesson. So I'm goin' to make it a hundred instead o' fifty."

The game wound up 3 to 1. The fine didn't go, because Ike hit like a wild man all through that trip and we made pretty near a clean-up. The night we went to Philly I got him cornered in the car and I says to him:

"Forget them alibis for a wile and tell me somethin'. What'd you do that for, swing that time against Marquard when you was told to bunt?"

"I'll tell you," he says. "That ball he throwed me looked just like the one I struck out on in the first innin' and I wanted to show Cap what I could of done to that other one if I'd knew it was the third strike."

"But," I says, "the one you struck out on in the first innin' was a fast ball."

"So was the one I cracked in the ninth," says Ike.

IV

You've saw Cap's wife, o' course. Well, her sister's about twict as good-lookin' as her, and that's goin' some.

Cap took his missus down to St. Louis the second trip and the other one come down from St. Joe to visit her. Her name is Dolly, and some doll is right.

Well, Cap was goin' to take the two sisters to a show and he wanted a beau for Dolly. He left it to her and she picked Ike. He'd hit three on the nose that afternoon—off'n Sallee, too.

They fell for each other that first evenin'. Cap told us how it come off. She begin flatterin' Ike for the star game he'd played and o' course he begin excusin' himself for not doin' better. So she thought he was modest and it went strong with her. And she believed everything he said and that made her solid with him—that and her make-up. They was together every mornin' and evenin' for the five days we was there. In the afternoons Ike played the grandest ball you ever see, hittin' and runnin' the bases like a fool and catchin' everything that stayed in the park.

I told Cap, I says: "You'd ought to keep the doll with us and he'd make Cobb's figures look sick."

But Dolly had to go back to St. Joe and we come home for a long serious.

Well, for the next three weeks Ike had a letter to read every day and he'd set in the clubhouse readin' it till mornin' practice was half over. Cap didn't say nothin' to him, because he was goin' so good. But I and Carey wasted a lot of our time tryin' to get him to own up who the letters was from. Fine chanct!

"What are you readin'?" Carey'd say. "A bill?"

"No," Ike'd say, "not exactly a bill. It's a letter from a fella I used to go to school with."

"High school or college?" I'd ask him.

"College," he'd say.

"What college?" I'd say.

Then he'd stall a wile and then he'd say:

"I didn't go to the college myself, but my friend went there."

"How did it happen you didn't go?" Carey'd ask him.

"Well," he'd say, "they wasn't no colleges near where I lived."

"Didn't you live in Kansas City?" I'd say to him.

One time he'd say he did and another time he didn't. One time he says he lived in Michigan.

"Where at? "says Carey.

"Near Detroit," he says.

"Well," I says, "Detroit's near Ann Arbor and that's where they got the university."

"Yes," says Ike, "they got it there now, but they didn't have it there then."

"I come pretty near goin' to Syracuse," I says, "only they wasn't no railroads runnin' through there in them days."

"Where'd this friend o' yours go to college?" says Carey.

"I forget now," says Ike.

"Was it Carlisle? "ast Carey.

"No," says Ike, "his folks wasn't very well off."

"That's what barred me from Smith," I says.

"I was goin' to tackle Cornell's," says Carey, "but the doctor told me I'd have hay fever if I didn't stay up North."

"Your friend writes long letters," I says.

"Yes," says Ike; "he's tellin' me about a ball player."

"Where does he play?" ast Carey.

"Down in the Texas League—Fort Wayne," says Ike.

"It looks like a girl's writin'," Carey says.

"A girl wrote it," says Ike. "That's my friend's sister, writin' for him."

"Didn't they teach writin' at this here college where he went?" says Carey.

"Sure," Ike says, "they taught writin', but he got his hand cut off in a railroad wreck."

"How long ago?" I says.

"Right after he got out o' college," says Ike.

"Well," I says, "I should think he'd of learned to write with his left hand by this time."

"It's his left hand that was cut off," says Ike; "and he was lefthanded."

"You get a letter every day," says Carey. "They're all the same writin'. Is he tellin' you about a different ball player every time he writes?"

"No," Ike says. "It's the same ball player. He just tells me what he does every day."

"From the size o' the letters, they don't play nothin' but double-headers down there," says Carey.

We figured that Ike spent most of his evenin's answerin' the letters from his "friend's sister," so we kept tryin' to date him up for shows and parties to see how he'd duck out of 'em. He was bugs over spaghetti, so we told him one day that they was goin' to be a big feed of it over to Joe's that night and he was invited.

"How long'll it last?" he says.

"Well," we says, "we're goin' right over there after the game and stay till they close up."

"I can't go," he says, "unless they leave me come home at eight bells."

"Nothin' doin'," says Carey. "Joe'd get sore."

"I can't go then," says Ike.

"Why not?" I ast him.

"Well," he says, "my landlady locks up the house at eight and I left my key home."

"You can come and stay with me," says Carey.

"No," he says, "I can't sleep in a strange bed."

"How do you get along when we're on the road?" says I.

"I don't never sleep the first night anywheres," he says. "After that I'm all right."

"You'll have time to chase home and get your key right after the game," I told him.

"The key ain't home," says Ike. "I lent it to one o' the other fellas and he's went out o' town and took it with him."

"Couldn't you borry another key off'n the landlady?" Carey ast him.

"No," he says, "that's the only one they is."

Well, the day before we started East again, Ike come into the clubhouse all smiles.

"Your birthday?" I ast him.

"No," he says.

"What do you feel so good about?" I says.

"Got a letter from my old man," he says. "My uncle's goin' to get well."

"Is that the one in Nebraska?" says I

"Not right in Nebraska," says Ike. "Near there."

But afterwards we got the right dope from Cap. Dolly'd blew in from Missouri and was goin' to make the trip with her sister.

V

Well, I want to alibi Carey and I for what come off in Boston. If we'd of had any idear what we was doin', we'd never did it. They wasn't nobody outside o' maybe Ike and the dame that felt worse over it than I and Carey.

The first two days we didn't see nothin' of Ike and her except out to the park. The rest o' the time they was sight-seein' over to Cambridge and down to Revere and out to Brook-a-line and all the other places where the rubes go.

But when we come into the beanery after the third game Cap's wife called us over.

"If you want to see somethin' pretty," she says, "look at the third finger on Sis's left hand."

Well, o' course we knowed before we looked that it wasn't goin' to be no hangnail. Nobody was su'prised when Dolly blew into the dinin' room with it—a rock that Ike'd bought off'n Diamond Joe the first trip to New York. Only o' course it'd been set into a lady's-size ring instead o' the automobile tire he'd been wearin'.

Cap and his missus and Ike and Dolly ett supper together, only Ike didn't eat nothin', but just set there blushin' and spillin' things on the table-cloth. I heard him excusin' himself for not havin' no appetite. He says he couldn't never eat when he was clost to the ocean. He'd forgot about them sixty-five oysters he destroyed the first night o' the trip before.

He was goin' to take her to a show, so after supper he went upstairs to change his collar. She had to doll up, too, and o' course Ike was through long before her.

If you remember the hotel in Boston, they's a little parlor. where the piano's at and then they's another little parlor openin' off o' that. Well, when Ike come down Smitty was playin' a few chords and I and Carey was harmonizin'. We seen Ike go up to the desk to leave his key and we called him in. He tried to duck away, but we wouldn't stand for it.

We ast him what he was all duded up for and he says he was goin' to the theayter.

"Goin' alone?" says Carey.

"No," he says, "a friend o' mine's goin' with me."

"What do you say if we go along?" says Carey.

"I ain't only got two tickets," he says.

"Well," says Carey, "we can go down there with you and buy our own seats maybe we can all get together."

"No," says Ike. "They ain't no more seats. They're all sold out."

"We can buy some off'n the scalpers," says Carey.

"I wouldn't if I was you," says Ike. "They say the show's rotten."

"What are you goin' for, then?" I ast.

"I didn't hear about it bein' rotten till I got the tickets," he says.

"Well," I says, "if you don't want to go I'll buy the tickets from you."

"No," says Ike, "I wouldn't want to cheat you. I'm stung and I'll just have to stand for it."

"What are you goin' to do with the girl, leave her here at the hotel?" I says.

"What girl?" says Ike.

"The girl you ett supper with," I says.

"Oh," he says, "we just happened to go into the dinin' room together, that's all. Cap wanted I should set down with 'em."

"I noticed." says Carey, "that she happened to he wearin' that rock you bought off'n Diamond Joe."

"Yes." says Ike. "I lent it to her for a wile."

"Did you lend her the new ring that goes with it?" I says.

"She had that already," says Ike. "She lost the set out of it."

"I wouldn't trust no strange girl with a rock o' mine," says Carey.

"Oh, I guess she's all right," Ike says. "Besides, I was tired o' the stone. When a girl asks you for somethin', what are you goin' to do?"

He started out toward the desk, but we flagged him.

"Wait a minute!" Carey says. "I got a bet with Sam here, and it's up to you to settle it."

"Well," says Ike, "make it snappy. My friend'll be here any minute."

"I bet," says Carey, "that you and that girl was engaged to be married."

"Nothin' to it," says Ike.

"Now look here," says Carey, "this is goin' to cost me real money if I lose. Cut out the alibi stuff and give it to us straight. Cap's wife just as good as told us you was roped."

Ike blushed like a kid.

"Well, boys," he says, "I may as well own up. You win, Carey."

"Yatta boy!" says Carey. "Congratulations!"

"You got a swell girl, Ike," I says.

"She's a peach," says Smitty.

"Well, I guess she's O. K.," says Ike. "I don't know much about girls."

"Didn't you never run round with 'em?" I says.

"Oh, yes, plenty of 'em," says Ike. "But I never seen none I'd fall for."

"That is, till you seen this one," says Carey.

"Well," says Ike, "this one's O. K., but I wasn't thinkin' about gettin' married yet a wile."

"Who done the askin'—her?" says Carey.

"Oh, no," says Ike, "but sometimes a man don't know what he's gettin' into. Take a good-lookin' girl, and a man gen'ally almost always does about what she wants him to."

"They couldn't no girl lasso me unless I wanted to be lassoed," says Smitty.

"Oh, I don't know," says Ike. "When a fella gets to feelin' sorry for one of 'em it's all off."

Well, we left him go after shakin' hands all round. But he didn't take Dolly to no show that night. Some time wile we was talkin' she'd came into that other parlor and she'd stood there and heard us. I don't know how much she heard. But it was enough. Dolly and Cap's missus took the midnight train for New York. And from there Cap's wife sent her on her way back to Missouri.

She'd left the ring and a note for Ike with the clerk. But we didn't ask Ike if the note was from his friend in Fort Wayne, Texas.

VI

When we'd came to Boston Ike was hittin' plain .397. When we got back home he'd fell off to pretty near nothin'. He hadn't drove one out o' the infield in any o' them other Eastern parks, and he didn't even give no excuse for it.

To show you how bad he was, he struck out three times in Brooklyn one day and never opened his trap when Cap ast him what was the matter. Before, if he'd whiffed oncet in a game he'd of wrote a book tellin' why.

Well, we dropped from first place to fifth in four weeks and we was still goin' down. I and Carey was about the only ones in the club that spoke to each other, and all as we did was remind ourself o' what a boner we'd pulled.

"It's goin' to beat us out o' the big money," says Carey.

"Yes," I says. "I don't want to knock my own ball club, but it looks like a one-man team, and when that one man's dauber's down we couldn't trim our whiskers."

"We ought to knew better," says Carey.

"Yes," I says, "but why should a man pull an alibi for bein' engaged to such a bearcat as she was?"

"He shouldn't," says Carey. "But I and you knowed he would or we'd never started talkin' to him about it. He wasn't no more ashamed o' the girl than I am of a regular base hit. But he just can't come clean on no subjec'."

Cap had the whole story, and I and Carey was as pop'lar with him as an umpire.

"What do you want me to do, Cap?" Carey'd say to him before goin' up to hit.

"Use your own judgment," Cap'd tell him. "We want to lose another game."

But finally, one night in Pittsburgh, Cap had a letter from his missus and he come to us with it.

"You fellas," he says, "is the ones that put us on the bum, and if you're sorry I think they's a chancet for you to make good. The old lady's out to St. Joe and she's been tryin' her hardest to fix things up. She's explained that Ike don't mean nothin' with his talk; I've wrote and explained that to Dolly, too. But the old lady says that Dolly says that she can't believe it. But Dolly's still stuck on this baby, and she's pinin' away just the same as Ike. And the old lady says she thinks if you two fellas would write to the girl and explain how you was always kiddin' with Ike and leadin' him on, and how the ball club was all shot to pieces since Ike quit hittin', and how he acted like he was goin' to kill himself, and this and that, she'd fall for it and maybe soften down. Dolly, the old lady says, would believe you before she'd believe I and the old lady, because she thinks it's her we're sorry for, and not him."

Well, I and Carey was only too glad to try and see what we could do. But it wasn't no snap. We wrote about eight letters before we got one that looked good. Then we give it to the stenographer and had it wrote out on a typewriter and both of us signed it.

It was Carey's idear that made the letter good. He stuck in somethin' about the world's serious money that our wives wasn't goin' to spend unless she took pity on a "boy who was so shy and modest that he was afraid to come right out and say that he had asked such a beautiful and handsome girl to become his bride."

That's prob'ly what got her, or maybe she couldn't of held out much longer anyway. It was four days after we sent the letter that Cap heard from his missus again. We was in Cincinnati.

"We've won," he says to us. "The old lady says that Dolly says she'll give him another chance. But the old lady says it won't do no good for Ike to write a letter. He'll have to go out there."

"Send him to-night," says Carey.

"I'll pay half his fare," I says.

"I'll pay the other half," says Carey.

"No," says Cap, "the club'll pay his expenses. I'll send him scoutin.'"

"Are you goin' to send him to-night?"

"Sure," says Cap. "But I'm goin' to break the news to him right now. It's time we win a ball game."

So in the clubhouse, just before the game, Cap told him. And I certainly felt sorry for Rube Benton and Red Ames that afternoon! I and Carey was standin' in front o' the hotel that night when Ike come out with his suitcase.

"Sent home?" I says to him.

"No," he says, "I'm goin' scoutin.'"

"Where to? " I says. "Fort Wayne?"

"No, not exactly," he says.

"Well," says Carey, "have a good time."

"I ain't lookin' for no good time," says Ike. "I says I was goin' scoutin'."

"Well, then," says Carey, "I hope you see somebody you like."

"And you better have a drink before you go," I says.

"Well," says Ike, "they claim it helps a cold."

Champion

Midge Kelly scored his first knockout when he was seventeen. The knockee was his brother Connie, three years his junior and a cripple. The purse was a half dollar given to the younger Kelly by a lady whose electric had just missed bumping his soul from his frail little body.

Connie did not know Midge was in the house, else he never would have risked laying the prize on the arm of the least comfortable chair in the room, the better to observe its shining beauty. As Midge entered from the kitchen, the crippled boy covered the coin with his hand, but the movement lacked the speed requisite to escape his brother's quick eye.

"Watcha got there?" demanded Midge.

"Nothin'," said Connie.

"You're a one legged liar!" said Midge.

He strode over to his brother's chair and grasped the hand that concealed the coin.

"Let loose!" he ordered.

Connie began to cry.

"Let loose and shut up your noise," said the elder, and jerked his brother's hand from the chair arm.

The coin fell onto the bare floor. Midge pounced on it. His weak mouth widened in a triumphant smile.

"Nothin', huh?" he said. "All right, if it's nothin' you don't want it."

"Give that back," sobbed the younger.

"I'll give you a red nose, you little sneak! Where'd you steal it?"

"I didn't steal it. It's mine. A lady give it to me after she pretty near hit me with a car."

"It's a crime she missed you," said Midge.

Midge started for the front door. The cripple picked up his crutch, rose from his chair with difficulty, and, still sobbing, came toward Midge. The latter heard him and stopped.

"You better stay where you're at," he said.

"I want my money," cried the boy.

"I know what you want," said Midge.

Doubling up the fist that held the half dollar, he landed with all his strength on his brother's mouth. Connie fell to the floor with a thud, the crutch tumbling on top of him. Midge stood beside the prostrate form.

"Is that enough?" he said. "Or do you want this, too?"

And he kicked him in the crippled leg.

"I guess that'll hold you," he said.

There was no response from the boy on the floor. Midge looked at him a moment, then at the coin in his hand, and then went out into the street, whistling.

An hour later, when Mrs. Kelly came home from her day's work at Faulkner's Steam Laundry, she found Connie on the floor, moaning. Dropping on her knees beside him, she called him by name a score of times. Then she got up and, pale as a ghost, dashed from the house. Dr. Ryan left the Kelly abode about dusk and walked toward Halsted Street. Mrs. Dorgan spied him as he passed her gate.

"Who's sick, Doctor?" she called.

"Poor little Connie," he replied. "He had a bad fall."

"How did it happen?"

"I can't say for sure, Margaret, but I'd almost bet he was knocked down."

"Knocked down!" exclaimed Mrs. Dorgan.

"Why, who—?"

"Have you seen the other one lately?"

"Michael? No, not since mornin'. You can't be thinkin'—"

"I wouldn't put it past him, Margaret," said the doctor gravely. "The lad's mouth is swollen and cut, and his poor, skinny little leg is bruised. He surely didn't do it to himself and I think Helen suspects the other one."

"Lord save us!" said Mrs. Dorgan. "I'll run over and see if I can help."

"That's a good woman," said Doctor Ryan, and went on down the street.

Near midnight, when Midge came home, his mother was sitting at Connie's bedside. She did not look up.

"Well," said Midge, "what's the matter?"

She remained silent. Midge repeated his question.

"Michael, you know what's the matter," she said at length.

"I don't know nothin'," said Midge.

"Don't lie to me, Michael. What did you do to your brother?"

"Nothin'."

"You hit him."

"Well, then, I hit him. What of it? It ain't the first time."

Her lips pressed tightly together, her face like chalk, Ellen Kelly rose from her chair and made straight for him. Midge backed against the door.

"Lay off'n me, Ma. I don't want to fight no woman."

Still she came on breathing heavily.

"Stop where you're at, Ma," he warned.

There was a brief struggle and Midge's mother lay on the floor before him.

"You ain't hurt, Ma. You're lucky I didn't land good. And I told you to lay off'n me."

"God forgive you, Michael!"

Midge found Hap Collins in the showdown game at the Royal.

"Come on out a minute," he said.

Hap followed him out on the walk.

"I'm leavin' town for a w'ile," said Midge.

"What for?"

"Well, we had a little run-in up to the house. The kid stole a half buck off'n me, and when I went after it he cracked me with his crutch. So I nailed him. And the old lady came at me with a chair and I took it off'n her and she fell down."

"How is Connie hurt?"

"Not bad."

"What are you runnin' away for?"

"Who the hell said I was runnin' away? I'm sick and tired o' gettin' picked on; that's all. So I'm leavin' for a w'ile and I want a piece o' money."

"I ain't only got six bits," said Happy.

"You're in bad shape, ain't you? Well, come through with it."

Happy came through.

"You oughtn't to hit the kid," he said.

"I ain't astin' you who can I hit," snarled Midge. "You try to put somethin' over on me and you'll get the same dose. I'm goin' now."

"Go as far as you like," said Happy, but not until he was sure that Kelly was out of hearing.

Early the following morning, Midge boarded a train for Milwaukee. He had no ticket, but no one knew the difference. The conductor remained in the caboose.

On a night six months later, Midge hurried out of the "stage door" of the Star Boxing Club and made for Duane's saloon, two blocks away. In his pocket were twelve dollars, his reward for having battered up one Demon Dempsey through the six rounds of the first preliminary.

It was Midge's first professional engagement in the manly art. Also it was the first time in weeks that he had earned twelve dollars.

On the way to Duane's he had to pass Niemann's. He pulled his cap over his eyes and increased his pace until he had gone by. Inside Niemann's stood a trusting bartender, who for ten days had staked Midge to drinks and allowed him to ravage the lunch on a promise to come in and settle the moment he was paid for the "prelim."

Midge strode into Duane's and aroused the napping bartender by slapping a silver dollar on the festive board.

"Gimme a shot," said Midge.

The shooting continued until the wind-up at the Star was over and part of the fight crowd joined Midge in front of Duane's bar. A youth in the early twenties, standing next to young Kelly, finally summoned sufficient courage to address him.

"Wasn't you in the first bout?" he ventured.

"Yeh," Midge replied.

"My name's Hersch," said the other.

Midge received the startling information in silence.

"I don't want to butt in," continued Mr. Hersch, "but I'd like to buy you a drink."

"All right," said Midge, "but don't overstrain yourself."

Mr. Hersch laughed uproariously and beckoned to the bartender.

"You certainly gave that wop a trimmin' tonight," said the buyer of the drink, when they had been served. "I thought you'd kill him."

"I would if I hadn't let up," Midge replied. "I'll kill 'em all."

"You got the wallop all right," the other said admiringly.

"Have I got the wallop?" said Midge. "Say, I can kick like a mule. Did you notice them muscles in my shoulders?"

"Notice 'em? I couldn't help from noticin' 'em," said Hersch. "I says to the fella settin' alongside o' me, I says: 'Look at them shoulders! No wonder he can hit,' I says to him."

"Just let me land and it's good-by, baby," said Midge. "I'll kill 'em all."

The oral manslaughter continued until Duane's closed for the night. At parting, Midge and his new friend shook hands and arranged for a meeting the following evening.

For nearly a week the two were together almost constantly. It was Hersch's pleasant rôle to listen to Midge's modest revelations concerning himself, and to buy every time Midge's glass was empty. But there came an evening when Hersch regretfully announced that he must go home to supper.

"I got a date for eight bells," he confided. "I could stick till then, only I must clean up and put on the Sunday clo'es, 'cause she's the prettiest little thing in Milwaukee."

"Can't you fix it for two?" asked Midge.

"I don't know who to get," Hersch replied. "Wait, though. I got a sister and if she ain't busy, it'll be O. K. She's no bum for looks herself."

So it came about that Midge and Emma Hersch and Emma's brother and the prettiest little thing in Milwaukee foregathered at Wall's and danced half the night away. And Midge and Emma danced every dance together, for though every little onestep seemed to induce a new thirst of its own, Lou Hersch stayed too sober to dance with his own sister.

The next day, penniless at last in spite of his phenomenal ability to make someone else settle, Midge Kelly sought out Doc Hammond, matchmaker for the Star, and asked to be booked for the next show.

"I could put you on with Tracy for the next bout," said Doc.

"What's they in it?" asked Midge.

"Twenty if you cop," Doc told him.

"Have a heart," protested Midge. "Didn't I look good the other night?"

"You looked all right. But you aren't Freddie Welsh yet by a consid'able margin."

"I ain't scared of Freddie Welsh or none of 'em," said Midge.

"Well, we don't pay our boxers by the size of their chests," Doc said. "I'm offerin' you this Tracy bout. Take it or leave it."

"All right; I'm on," said Midge, and he passed a pleasant afternoon at Duane's on the strength of his booking.

Young Tracy's manager came to Midge the night before the show.

"How do you feel about this go?" he asked.

"Me?" said Midge, "I feel all right. What do you mean, how do I feel?"

"I mean," said Tracy's manager, "that we're mighty anxious to win, 'cause the boy's got a chanct in Philly if he cops this one."

"What's your proposition?" asked Midge.

"Fifty bucks," said Tracy's manager.

"What do you think I am, a crook? Me lay down for fifty bucks. Not me!"

"Seventy-five, then," said Tracy's manager.

The market closed on eighty and the details were agreed on in short order. And the next night Midge was stopped in the second round by a terrific slap on the forearm.

This time Midge passed up both Niemann's and Duane's, having a sizable account at each place, and sought his refreshment at Stein's farther down the street.

When the profits of his deal with Tracy were gone, he learned, by first-hand information from Doc Hammond and the matchmakers at the other "clubs," that he was no longer desired for even the cheapest of preliminaries. There was no danger of his starving or dying of thirst while Emma and Lou Hersch lived. But he made up his mind, four months after his defeat by Young Tracy, that Milwaukee was not the ideal place for him to live.

"I can lick the best of 'em," he reasoned, "but there ain't no more chanct for me here. I can maybe go east and get on somewheres. And besides—"

But just after Midge had purchased a ticket to Chicago with the money he had "borrowed" from Emma Hersch "to buy shoes," a heavy hand was laid on his shoulders and he turned to face two strangers.

"Where are you goin', Kelly?" inquired the owner of the heavy hand.

"Nowheres," said Midge. "What the hell do you care?"

The other stranger spoke:

"Kelly, I'm employed by Emma Hersch's mother to see that you do right by her. And we want you to stay here till you've done it."

"You won't get nothin' but the worst of it, monkeying with me," said Midge.

Nevertheless, he did not depart for Chicago that night. Two days later, Emma Hersch became Mrs. Kelly, and the gift of the groom, when once they were alone, was a crushing blow on the bride's pale cheek.

Next morning, Midge left Milwaukee as he had entered it—by fast freight.

"They's no use kiddin' ourself any more," said Tommy Haley. "He might get down to thirty-seven in a pinch, but if he done below that a mouse could stop him. He's a welter; that's what he is and he knows it as well as I do. He's growed like a weed in the last six mont's. I told him, I says, 'If you don't quit growin' they won't be nobody for you to box, only Willard and them.' He says, 'Well, I wouldn't run away from Willard if I weighed twenty pounds more.' "

"He must hate himself," said Tommy's brother.

"I never seen a good one that didn't," said Tommy. "And Midge is a good one; don't make no mistake about that. I wisht we could of got Welsh before the kid growed so big. But it's too late now. I won't make no holler, though, if we can match him up with the Dutchman."

"Who do you mean?"

"Young Goetz, the welter champ. We mightn't not get so much dough for the bout itself, but it'd roll in afterward. What a drawin' card we'd be, 'cause the people pays their money to see the fella with the wallop, and that's Midge. And we'd keep the title just as long as Midge could make the weight."

"Can't you land no match with Goetz?"

"Sure, 'cause he needs the money. But I've went careful with the kid so far and look at the results I got! So what's the use of takin' a chanct? The kid's comin' every minute and Goetz is goin' back faster'n big Johnson did. I think we could lick him now; I'd bet my life on it. But six mont's from now they won't be no risk. He'll of licked hisself before that time. Then all as we'll have to do is sign up with him and wait for the referee to stop it. But Midge is so crazy to get at him now that I can't hardly hold him back."

The brothers Haley were lunching in a Boston hotel. Dan had come down from Holyoke to visit with Tommy and to watch the latter's protégé go twelve rounds, or less, with Bud Cross. The bout promised little in the way of a contest, for Midge had twice stopped the Baltimore youth and Bud's reputation for gameness was all that had earned him the date. The fans were willing to pay the price to see Midge's hay-making left, but they wanted to see it used on an opponent who would not jump out of the ring the first time he felt its crushing force. But Cross was such an opponent, and his willingness to stop boxing-gloves with his eyes, ears, nose and throat had long enabled him to escape the horrors of honest labor. A game boy was Bud, and he showed it in his battered, swollen, discolored face.

"I should think," said Dan Haley, "that the kid'd do whatever you tell him after all you done for him."

"Well," said Tommy, "he's took my dope pretty straight so far, but he's so sure of hisself that he can't see no reason for waitin'. He'll do what I say, though; he'd be a sucker not to."

"You got a contrac' with him?"

"No, I don't need no contrac'. He knows it was me that drug him out o' the gutter and he ain't goin' to turn me down now, when he's got the dough and bound to get more. Where'd he of been at if I hadn't listened to him when he first come to me? That's pretty near two years ago now, but it seems like last week. I was settin' in the s'loon acrost from the Pleasant Club in Philly, waitin' for McCann to count the dough and come over, when this little bum blowed in and tried to stand the house off for a drink. They told him nothin' doin' and to beat it out o' there, and then he seen me and come over to where I was settin' and ast me wasn't I a boxin' man and I told him who I was. Then he ast me for money to buy a shot and I told him to set down and I'd buy it for him.

"Then we got talkin' things over and he told me his name and told me about fightn' a couple o' prelims out to Milwaukee. So I says, 'Well, boy, I don't know how good or how rotten you are, but you won't never get nowheres trainin' on that stuff.' So he says he'd cut it out if he could get on in a bout and I says I would give him a chanct if he played square with me and didn't touch no more to drink. So we shook hands and I took him up to the hotel with me and give him a bath and the next day I bought him some clo'es. And I staked him to eats and sleeps for over six weeks. He had a hard time breakin' away from the polish, but finally I thought he was fit and I give him his chanct. He went on with Smiley Sayer and stopped him so quick that Smiley thought sure he was poisoned.

"Well, you know what he's did since. The only beatin' in his record was by Tracy in Milwaukee before I got hold of him, and he's licked Tracy three times in the last year.

"I've gave him all the best of it in a money way and he's got seven thousand bucks in cold storage. How's that for a kid that was in the gutter two years ago? And he'd have still more yet if he wasn't so nuts over clo'es and got to stop at the good hotels and so forth."

"Where's his home at?"

"Well, he ain't really got no home. He came from Chicago and his mother canned him out o' the house for bein' no good. She give him a raw deal, I guess, and he says he won't have nothin' to do with her unlest she comes to him first. She's got a pile o' money, he says, so he ain't worryin' about her."

The gentleman under discussion entered the café and swaggered to Tommy's table, while the whole room turned to look.

Midge was the picture of health despite a slightly colored eye and an ear that seemed to have no opening. But perhaps it was not his healthiness that drew all eyes. His diamond horse-shoe tie pin, his purple cross-striped shirt, his orange shoes and his light blue suit fairly screamed for attention.

"Where you been?" he asked Tommy. "I been lookin' all over for you."

"Set down," said his manager.

"No time," said Midge. "I'm goin' down to the w'arf and see 'em unload the fish."

"Shake hands with my brother Dan," said Tommy.

Midge shook with the Holyoke Haley.

"If you're Tommy's brother, you're O. K. with me," said Midge, and the brothers beamed with pleasure.

Dan moistened his lips and murmured an embarrassed reply, but it was lost on the young gladiator.

"Leave me take twenty," Midge was saying. "I prob'ly won't need it, but I don't like to be caught short."

Tommy parted with a twenty dollar bill and recorded the transaction in a small black book the insurance company had given him for Christmas.

"But," he said, "it won't cost you no twenty to look at them fish. Want me to go along?"

"No," said Midge hastily. "You and your brother here prob'ly got a lot to say to each other."

"Well," said Tommy, "don't take no bad money and don't get lost. And you better be back at four o'clock and lay down a w'ile."

"I don't need no rest to beat this guy," said Midge. "He'll do enough layin' down for the both of us."

And laughing even more than the jest called for, he strode out through the fire of admiring and startled glances.

The corner of Boylston and Tremont was the nearest Midge got to the wharf, but the lady awaiting him was doubtless a more dazzling sight than the catch of the luckiest Massachusetts fisherman. She could talk, too—probably better than the fish.

"O you Kid!" she said, flashing a few silver teeth among the gold. "O you fighting man!"

Midge smiled up at her.

"We'll go somewheres and get a drink," he said. "One won't hurt."

In New Orleans, five months after he had rearranged the map of Bud Cross for the third time, Midge finished training for his championship bout with the Dutchman.

Back in his hotel after the final workout, Midge stopped to chat with some of the boys from up north, who had made the long trip to see a champion dethroned, for the result of this bout was so nearly a foregone conclusion that even the experts had guessed it.

Tommy Haley secured the key and the mail and ascended to the Kelly suite. He was bathing when Midge came in, half an hour later.

"Any mail?" asked Midge.

"There on the bed," replied Tommy from the tub.

Midge picked up the stack of letters and postcards and glanced them over. From the pile he sorted out three letters and laid them on the table. The rest he tossed into the waste-basket. Then he picked up the three and sat for a few moments holding them, while his eyes gazed off into space. At length he looked again at the three unopened letters in his hand; then he put one in his pocket and tossed the other two at the basket. They missed their target and fell on the floor.

"Hell!" said Midge, and stooping over picked them up.

He opened one postmarked Milwaukee and read:

Dear Husband:

I have wrote to you so manny times and got no anser and I dont know if you ever got them, so I am writeing again in the hopes you will get this letter and anser. I dont like to bother you with my trubles and I would not only for the baby and I am not asking you should write to me but only send a little money and I am not asking for myself but the baby has *not been well a day sence last Aug. and the dr. told me she cant live much longer unless I give her better food and thats impossible the way things are. Lou has not been working for a year and what I make dont hardley pay for the rent. I am not asking for you to give me any money, but only you should send what I loaned when convenient and I think it amts. to about $36.00. Please try and send that amt. and it will help me, but if you cant send the whole amt. try and send me something.*

Your wife,
Emma.

Midge tore the letter into a hundred pieces and scattered them over the floor.

"Money, money, money!" he said. "They must think I'm made o' money. I s'pose the old woman's after it too."

He opened his mother's letter:

Dear Michael Connie wonted me to rite and say you must beet the dutchman and he is sur you will and wonted me to say we wont you to rite and tell us about it, but I gess you havent no time to rite or we herd from you long beffore this but I wish you would rite jest a line or 2 boy becaus it wuld be better for Connie then a barl of medisin. It wuld help me to keep things going if you send me money now and then when you can spair it but if you cant send no money try and fine time to rite a letter onley a few lines and it will please Connie. jest think boy he hasent got out of bed in over 3 yrs. Connie says good luck.

Your Mother,
Ellen F. Kelly.

"I thought so," said Midge. "They're all alike."
The third letter was from New York. It read:

Hon:—This is the last letter you will get from me before your champ, but I will send you a telegram Saturday, but I can't say as much in a telegram as in a letter and I am writeing this to let you know I am thinking of you and praying for good luck.

Lick him good hon and don't wait no longer than you have to and don't forget to wire me as soon as its over. Give him that little old left of yours on the nose hon and don't be afraid of spoiling his good looks because he couldn't be no homlier than he is. But don't let him spoil my baby's pretty face. You won't will you hon.

Well hon I would give anything to be there and see it, but I guess you love Haley better than me or you wouldn't let him keep me away. But when your champ hon we can do as we please and tell Haley to go to the devil.

Well hon I will send you a telegram Saturday and I almost forgot to tell you I will need some more money, a couple hundred say and you will have to wire it to me as soon as you get this. You will won't you hon.

I will send you a telegram Saturday and remember hon I am pulling for you.

Well good-by sweetheart and good luck.

Grace.

"They're all alike," said Midge. "Money, money, money."

Tommy Haley, shining from his ablutions, came in from the adjoining room.

"Thought you'd be layin' down," he said.

"I'm goin' to," said Midge, unbuttoning his orange shoes.

"I'll call you at six and you can eat up here without no bugs to pester you. I got to go down and give them birds their tickets."

"Did you hear from Goldberg?" asked Midge.

"Didn't I tell you? Sure; fifteen weeks at five hundred, if we win. And we can get a guarantee o' twelve thousand, with privileges either in New York or Milwaukee."

"Who with?"

"Anybody that'll stand up in front of you. You don't care who it is, do you?"

"Not me. I'll make 'em all look like a monkey."

"Well you better lay down aw'ile."

"Oh, say, wire two hundred to Grace for me, will you? Right away; the New York address."

"Two hundred! You just sent her three hundred last Sunday."

"Well, what the hell do you care?"

"All right, all right. Don't get sore about it. Anything else?"

"That's all," said Midge, and dropped onto the bed.

"And I want the deed done before I come back," said Grace as she rose from the table. "You won't fall down on me, will you, hon?"

"Leave it to me," said Midge. "And don't spend no more than you have to."

Grace smiled a farewell and left the café. Midge continued to sip his coffee and read his paper.

They were in Chicago and they were in the middle of Midge's first week in vaudeville. He had come straight north to reap the rewards of his glorious victory over the broken down Dutchman. A fortnight had been spent in learning his act, which consisted of a gymnastic exhibition and a ten minutes' monologue on the various excellences of Midge Kelly. And now he was twice daily turning 'em away from the Madison Theater.

His breakfast over and his paper read, Midge sauntered into the lobby and asked for his key. He then beckoned to a bell-boy, who had been hoping for that very honor.

"Find Haley, Tommy Haley," said Midge. "Tell him to come up to my room."

"Yes, sir, Mr. Kelly," said the boy, and proceeded to break all his former records for diligence.

Midge was looking out of his seventh-story window when Tommy answered the summons.

"What'll it be?" inquired his manager.

There was a pause before Midge replied.

"Haley," he said, "twenty-five per cent's a whole lot o' money."

"I guess I got it comin', ain't I?" said Tommy.

"I don't see how you figger it. I don't see where you're worth it to me."

"Well," said Tommy, "I didn't expect nothin' like this. I thought you was satisfied with the bargain. I don't want to beat nobody out o' nothin', but I don't see where you could have got anybody else that would of did all I done for you."

"Sure, that's all right," said the champion. "You done a lot for me in Philly. And you got good money for it, didn't you?"

"I ain't makin' no holler. Still and all, the big money's still ahead of us yet. And if it hadn't of been for me, you wouldn't of never got within grabbin' distance."

"Oh, I guess I could of went along all right," said Midge. "Who was it that hung that left on the Dutchman's jaw, me or you?"

"Yes, but you wouldn't been in the ring with the Dutchman if it wasn't for how I handled you."

"Well, this won't get us nowheres. The idear is that you ain't worth no twenty-five per cent now and it don't make no diff'rence what come off a year or two ago."

"Don't it?" said Tommy. "I'd say it made a whole lot of diference."

"Well, I say it don't and I guess that settles it."

"Look here, Midge," Tommy said, "I thought I was fair with you, but if you don't think so, I'm willin' to hear what you think is fair. I don't want nobody callin' me a Sherlock. Let's go down to business and sign up a contrac'. What's your figger?"

"I ain't namin' no figger," Midge replied. "I'm sayin' that twenty-five's too much. Now what are you willin' to take?"

"How about twenty?"

"Twenty's too much," said Kelly.

"What ain't too much?" asked Tommy.

"Well, Haley, I might as well give it to you straight. They ain't nothin' that ain't too much."

"You mean you don't want me at no figger?"

"That's the idear."

There was a minute's silence. Then Tommy Haley walked toward the door.

"Midge," he said, in a choking voice, "you're makin' a big mistake, boy. You can't throw down your best friends and get away with it. That damn woman will ruin you."

Midge sprang from his seat.

"You shut your mouth!" he stormed. "Get out o' here before they have to carry you out. You been spongin' off o' me long enough. Say one more word about the girl or about anything else and you'll get what the Dutchman got. Now get out!"

And Tommy Haley, having a very vivid memory of the Dutchman's face as he fell, got out.

Grace came in later, dropped her numerous bundles on the lounge and perched herself on the arm of Midge's chair.

"Well?" she said.

"Well," said Midge, "I got rid of him."

"Good boy!" said Grace. "And now I think you might give me that twenty-five per cent."

"Besides the seventy-five you're already gettin'?" said Midge.

"Don't be no grouch, hon. You don't look pretty when you're grouchy."

"It ain't my business to look pretty," Midge replied.

"Wait till you see how I look with the stuff I bought this mornin'!"

Midge glanced at the bundles on the lounge.

"There's Haley's twenty-five per cent," he said, "and then some."

The champion did not remain long without a manager. Haley's successor was none other than Jerome Harris, who saw in Midge a better meal ticket than his popular-priced musical show had been.

The contract, giving Mr. Harris twenty-five per cent of Midge's earnings, was signed in Detroit the week after Tommy Haley had heard his dismissal read. It had taken Midge just six days to learn that a popular actor cannot get on without the ministrations of a man who thinks, talks and means business. At first Grace objected to the new member of the firm, but when Mr. Harris had demanded and secured from the vaudeville people a one-hundred dollar increase in Midge's weekly stipend, she was convinced that the champion had acted for the best.

"You and my missus will have some great old times," Harris told Grace. "I'd of wired her to join us here, only I seen the Kid's bookin' takes us to Milwaukee next week, and that's where she is."

But when they were introduced in the Milwaukee hotel, Grace admitted to herself that her feeling for Mrs. Harris could hardly be called love at first sight. Midge, on the contrary, gave his new manager's wife the many times over and seemed loath to end the feast of his eyes.

"Some doll," he said to Grace when they were alone.

"Doll is right," the lady replied, "and sawdust where her brains ought to be."

"I'm li'ble to steal that baby," said Midge, and he smiled as he noted the effect of his words on his audience's face.

On Tuesday of the Milwaukee week the champion successfully defended his title in a bout that the newspapers never reported. Midge was alone in his room that morning when a visitor entered without knocking. The visitor was Lou Hersch.

Midge turned white at sight of him.

"What do you want?" he demanded.

"I guess you know," said Lou Hersch. "Your wife's starvin' to death and your baby's starvin' to death and I'm starvin' to death. And you're dirty with money."

"Listen," said Midge, "if it wasn't for you, I wouldn't never saw your sister. And, if you ain't man enough to hold a job, what's that to me? The best thing you can do is keep away from me."

"You give me a piece o' money and I'll go."

Midge's reply to the ultimatum was a straight right to his brother-in-law's narrow chest.

"Take that home to your sister."

And after Lou Hersch had picked himself up and slunk away, Midge thought: "It's lucky I didn't give him my left or I'd of croaked him. And if I'd hit him in the stomach, I'd of broke his spine."

There was a party after each evening performance during the Milwaukee engagement. The wine flowed freely and Midge had more of it than Tommy Haley ever would have permitted him. Mr. Harris offered no objection, which was possibly just as well for his own physical comfort.

In the dancing between drinks, Midge had his new manager's wife for a partner as often as Grace. The latter's face as she floundered round in the arms of the portly Harris, belied her frequent protestations that she was having the time of her life.

Several times that week, Midge thought Grace was on the point of starting the quarrel he hoped to have. But it was not until Friday night that she accommodated. He and Mrs. Harris had disappeared after the matinee and when Grace saw him again at the close of the night show, she came to the point at once.

"What are you tryin' to pull off?" she demanded.

"It's none o' your business, is it?" said Midge.

"You bet it's my business; mine and Harris's. You cut it short or you'll find out."

"Listen," said Midge, "have you got a mortgage on me or somethin'? You talk like we was married."

"We're goin' to be, too. And to-morrow's as good a time as any."

"Just about," Midge said. "You got as much chanct o' marryin' me to-morrow as the next day or next year and that ain't no chanct at all."

"We'll find out," said Grace.

"You're the one that's got somethin' to find out."

"What do you mean?"

"I mean I'm married already."

"You lie!"

"You think so, do you? Well, s'pose you go to this here address and get acquainted with my missus."

Midge scrawled a number on a piece of paper and handed it to her. She stared at it unseeingly.

"Well," said Midge, "I ain't kiddin' you. You go there and ask for Mrs. Michael Kelly, and if you don't find her, I'll marry you to-morrow before breakfast."

Still Grace stared at the scrap of paper. To Midge it seemed an age before she spoke again.

"You lied to me all this w'ile."

"You never ast me was I married. What's more, what the hell diff'rence did it make to you? You got a split, didn't you? Better'n fifty-fifty."

He started away.

"Where you goin'?"

"I'm goin' to meet Harris and his wife."

"I'm goin' with you. You're not goin' to shake me now."

"Yes, I am, too," said Midge quietly. "When I leave town to-morrow night, you're going to stay here. And if I see where you're goin' to make a fuss, I'll put you in a hospital where they'll keep you quiet. You can get your stuff to-morrow mornin' and I'll slip you a hundred bucks. And then I don't want to see no more o' you. And don't try and tag along now or I'll have to add another K. O. to the old record."

When Grace returned to the hotel that night, she discovered that Midge and the Harrises had moved to another. And when Midge left town the following night, he was again without a manager, and Mr. Harris was without a wife.

Three days prior to Midge Kelly's ten-round bout with Young Milton in New York City, the sporting editor of *The News* assigned Joe Morgan to write two or three thousand words about the champion to run with a picture lay-out for Sunday.

Joe Morgan dropped in at Midge's training quarters Friday afternoon. Midge, he learned, was doing road work, but Midge's manager, Wallie Adams, stood ready and willing to supply reams of dope about the greatest fighter of the age.

"Let's hear what you've got," said Joe, "and then I'll try to fix up something."

So Wallie stepped on the accelerator of his imagination and shot away.

"Just a kid; that's all he is; a regular boy. Get what I mean? Don't know the meanin' o' bad habits. Never tasted liquor in his life and would prob'bly get sick if he smelled it. Clean livin' put him up where he's at. Get what I mean? And modest and unassumin' as a school girl. He's so quiet you wouldn't never know he was round. And he'd go to jail before he'd talk about himself.

"No job at all to get him in shape, 'cause he's always that way. The only trouble we have with him is gettin' him to light into these poor bums they match him up with. He's scared he'll hurt somebody. Get what I mean? He's tickled to death over this match with Milton, 'cause everybody says Milton can stand the gaff. Midge'll maybe be able to cut loose a little this time. But the last two bouts he had, the guys hadn't no business in the ring with him, and he was holdin' back all the w'ile for the fear he'd kill somebody. Get what I mean?"

"Is he married?" inquired Joe.

"Say, you'd think he was married to hear him rave about them kiddies he's got. His fam'ly's up in Canada to their summer home and Midge is wild to get up there with 'em. He thinks more o' that wife and them kiddies than all the money in the world. Get what I mean?"

"How many children has he?"

"I don't know, four or five, I guess. All boys and every one of 'em a dead ringer for their dad."

"Is his father living?"

"No, the old man died when he was a kid. But he's got a grand old mother and a kid brother out in Chi. They're the first ones he thinks about after a match, them and his wife and kiddies. And he don't forget to send the old woman a thousand bucks after every bout. He's goin' to buy her a new home as soon as they pay him off for this match."

"How about his brother? Is he going to tackle the game?"

"Sure, and Midge says he'll be a champion before he's twenty years old. They're a fightin' fam'ly and all of 'em honest and straight as a die. Get what I mean? A fella that I can't tell you his name come to Midge in Milwaukee onct and wanted him to throw a fight and Midge give him such a trimmin' in the street that he couldn't go on that night. That's the kind he is. Get what I mean?"

Joe Morgan hung around the camp until Midge and his trainers returned.

"One o' the boys from *The News*," said Wallie by way of introduction. "I been givin' him your fam'ly hist'ry."

"Did he give you good dope?" he inquired.

"He's some historian," said Joe.

"Don't call me no names," said Wallie smiling. "Call us up if they's anything more you want. And keep your eyes on us Monday night. Get what I mean?"

The story in Sunday's *News* was read by thousands of lovers of the manly art. It was well written and full of human interest. Its slight inaccuracies went unchallenged, though three readers, besides Wallie

Adams and Midge Kelly, saw and recognized them. The three were Grace, Tommy Haley and Jerome Harris and the comments they made were not for publication.

Neither the Mrs. Kelly in Chicago nor the Mrs. Kelly in Milwaukee knew that there was such a paper as the New York *News*. And even if they had known of it and that it contained two columns of reading matter about Midge, neither mother nor wife could have bought it. For *The News* on Sunday is a nickel a copy.

Joe Morgan could have written more accurately, no doubt, if instead of Wallie Adams, he had interviewed Ellen Kelly and Connie Kelly and Emma Kelly and Lou Hersch and Grace and Jerome Harris and Tommy Haley and Hap Collins and two or three Milwaukee bartenders.

But a story built on their evidence would never have passed the sporting editor.

"Suppose you can prove it," that gentleman would have said, "It wouldn't get us anything but abuse to print it. The people don't want to see him knocked. He's champion."

Bonus content

Ring, by F. Scott Fitzgerald[1]

Published in The New Republic magazine (11 October 1933).

For a year and a half the writer of this appreciation was Ring Lardner's most familiar companion; after that, geography made separations and our contacts were rare. When my wife and I last saw him in 1931, he looked already like a man on his deathbed—it was terribly sad to see that six feet three inches of kindness stretched out ineffectual in the hospital room. His fingers trembled with a match, the tight skin on his handsome skull was marked as a mask of misery and nervous pain.

---

[1] Francis Scott Key Fitzgerald (September 24, 1896 – December 21, 1940) was an American novelist, essayist, and short story writer. He is best known for his novels depicting the flamboyance and excess of the Jazz Age—a term he popularized in his short story collection Tales of the Jazz Age. During his lifetime, he published four novels, four story collections, and 164 short stories. Although he achieved temporary popular success and fortune in the 1920s, Fitzgerald received critical acclaim only after his death and is now widely regarded as one of the greatest American writers of the 20th century.

He gave a very different impression when we first saw him in 1921—he seemed to have an abundance of quiet vitality that would enable him to outlast anyone, to take himself for long spurts of work or play that would ruin any ordinary constitution. He had recently convulsed the country with the famous kitten-and-coat saga (it had to do with a world's series bet and with the impending conversion of some kittens into fur), and the evidence of the betting, a beautiful sable, was worn by his wife at the time. In those days he was interested in people, sports, bridge, music, the stage, the newspapers, the magazines, the books. But though I did not know it, the change in him had already begun—the impenetrable despair that dogged him for a dozen years to his death.

He had practically given up sleeping, save on short vacations deliberately consecrated to simple pleasures, most frequently golf with his friends, Grantland Rice or John Wheeler. Many a night we talked over a case of Canadian ale until bright dawn, when Ring would rise and yawn: "Well, I guess the children have left for school by this time—I might as well go home."

The woes of many people haunted him—for example, the doctor's death sentence pronounced upon Tad, the cartoonist (who, in fact, nearly outlived Ring)—it was as if he believed he could and ought to do something about such things. And as he struggled to fulfil his contracts, one of which, a comic strip based on the character of "the busher", was a terror, indeed, it was obvious that he felt his work to be directionless, merely "copy". So he was inclined to turn his cosmic sense of responsibility into the channel of solving other people's problems—finding someone an introduction to a theatrical manager, placing a friend in a job, manoeuvring a man into a good club. The effort made was often out of proportion to the situation; the truth back of it was that Ring was getting off—he was a faithful and conscientious workman to the end, but he had stopped finding any fun in his work ten years before he died.

About that time (1922) a publisher undertook to reissue his old books and collect his recent stories and this gave him a sense of existing in the literary world as well as with the public, and he got some satisfaction from the reiterated statements of Mencken and F.P.A. as to his true stature as a writer. But I don't think he cared then—it is hard to understand, but I don't think he really gave a damn about anything except his personal relations with a few people. A case in point was his attitude to those imitators who lifted everything except the shirt off his back—only Hemingway has been so thoroughly frisked—it worried the imitators more than it worried Ring. His attitude was that if they got stuck in the process he'd help them over any tough place.

Throughout this period of huge earnings and an increasingly solid reputation on top and beneath, there were two ambitions more important to Ring than the work by which he will be remembered; he wanted to be a musician—sometimes he dramatized himself ironically as a thwarted composer—and he wanted to write shows. His dealings with managers would make a whole story: they were always commissioning him to do work which they promptly forgot they had ordered, and accepting librettos that they never produced. (Ring left a short ironic record of Ziegfeld.) Only with the aid of the practical George Kaufman did he achieve his ambition, and by then he was too far gone in illness to get a proper satisfaction from it.

The point of these paragraphs is that, whatever Ring's achievement was, it fell short of the achievement he was capable of, and this because of a cynical attitude towards his work. How far back did that attitude go?—back to his youth in a Michigan village? Certainly back to his days with the Cubs. During those years, when most men of promise achieve an adult education, if only in the school of war, Ring moved in the company of a few dozen illiterates playing a boy's game. A boy's game, with no more possibilities in it than a boy could master, a game bounded by walls which kept out novelty or danger, change or adventure. This material, the observation of it under such circumstances, was the text of Ring's schooling during the most formative period of the mind. A writer can spin on about his adventures after thirty, after forty, after fifty, but the criteria by which these adventures are weighed and valued are irrevocably settled at the age of twenty-five. However deeply Ring might cut into it, his cake had exactly the diameter of Frank Chance's diamond.

Here was his artistic problem, and it promised future trouble. So long as he wrote within that enclosure the result was magnificent: within it he heard and recorded the voice of a continent. But when, inevitably, he outgrew his interest in it, what was Ring left with?

He was left with his fine ethymological technique—and he was left rather helpless in those few acres. He had been formed by the very world on which his hilarious irony had released itself. He had fought his way through to knowing what people's motives are and what means they are likely to resort to in order to attain their goals. But now he had a new problem—what to do about it. He went on seeing, and the sights travelled back to the optic nerve, but no longer to be thrown off in fiction, because they were no longer sights that could be weighed and valued by the old criteria. It was never that he was completely sold on athletic virtuosity as the be-all and end-all of problems; the trouble was that he could find nothing finer. Imagine life conceived as a business of beautiful muscular organization—an arising, an effort, a good break, a sweat, a bath, a meal, a love, a sleep—imagine it achieved; then imagine trying to apply that standard to the horribly complicated mess of living, where nothing, even the greatest conceptions and workings and achievements, is else but messy, spotty, tortuous—and then one can imagine the confusion that Ring faced on coming out of the ball park.

He kept on recording but he no longer projected, and this accumulation, which he has taken with him to the grave, crippled his spirit in the latter years. It was not the fear of Niles, Michigan, that hampered him—it was the habit of silence, formed in the presence of the "ivory" with which he lived and worked. Remember it was not humble ivory—Ring has demonstrated that—it was arrogant, imperative, often megalomaniacal ivory. He got the habit of silence, then the habit of repression that finally took the form of his odd little crusade in "The New Yorker" against pornographic songs. He had agreed with himself to speak only a small portion of his mind.

The present writer once suggested to him that he organize some *cadre* within which he could adequately display his talents, suggesting that it should be something deeply personal, and something on which Ring could take his time, but he dismissed the idea lightly; he was a disillusioned idealist but he had served his Fates well, and no other ones could be casually created for him—"This is something that can be printed," he reasoned. "This, however, must join that accumulated mass of reflections that can never be written."

He covered himself in such cases with protests of his inability to bring off anything big, but this was specious, for he was a proud man and had no reason to rate his abilities cheaply. He refused to "tell all" because in a crucial period of his life he had formed the habit of not doing it—and this he had elevated gradually into a standard of taste. It never satisfied him by a damn sight.

So one is haunted not only by a sense of personal loss but by a conviction that Ring got less percentage of himself on paper than any other American of the first flight. There is "You Know Me, Al", and there are about a dozen wonderful short stories (my God, he hadn't even saved them—the material of "How to Write Short Stories" was obtained by photographing old issues in the public library!), and there is some of the most uproarious and inspired nonsense since Lewis Carroll. Most of the rest is mediocre stuff, with flashes, and I would do Ring a disservice to suggest it should be set upon an altar and worshipped, as have been the most casual relics of Mark Twain. Those three volumes should seem enough—to everyone who didn't know Ring. But I venture that no one who knew him but will agree that the personality of the man overlapped it. Proud, shy, solemn, shrewd, polite, brave, kind, merciful, honourable—with the affection these qualities aroused he created in addition a certain awe in people. His intentions, his will, once in motion, were formidable factors in dealing with him—he always did every single thing he said he would do. Frequently he was the melancholy Jaques, and sad company indeed, but under any conditions a noble dignity flowed from him, so that time in his presence always seemed well spent.

On my desk, at the moment, I have the letters Ring wrote to us; here is a letter one thousand words long, here is one of two thousand words—theatrical gossip, literary shop talk, flashes of wit but not much wit, for he was feeling thin and saving the best of that for his work, anecdotes of his activities. I reprint the most typical one I can find:

"The Dutch Treat show was a week ago Friday night. Grant Rice and I had reserved a table, and a table holds ten people and no more. Well, I had invited, as one guest, Jerry Kern, but he telephoned at the last moment that he couldn't come. I then consulted with Grant Rice, who said he had no substitute in mind, but that it was a shame to waste our extra ticket when tickets were at a premium. So I called up Jones, and Jones said yes, and would it be all right for him to bring along a former Senator who was a pal of his and had been good to him in Washington. I said I was sorry, but our table was filled and, besides, we didn't have an extra ticket. "Maybe I could dig up another ticket somewhere," said Jones. "I don't believe so," I said, "but anyway the point is that we haven't room at our table." "Well," said Jones, "I could have the Senator eat somewhere else and join us in time for the show." "Yes," I said, "but we have no ticket for him." "Well, I'll think up something," he said. Well, what he thought up was to bring himself and the Senator and I had a hell of a time getting an extra ticket and shoving the Senator in at another table where he wasn't wanted, and later in the evening, the Senator thanked Jones and said he was the greatest fella in the world and all I got was goodnight.

"Well, I must close and nibble on a carrot. R.W.L."

Even in a telegram Ring could compress a lot of himself. Here is one: WHEN ARE YOU COMING BACK AND WHY PLEASE ANSWER RING LARDNER.

This is not the moment to recollect Ring's convivial aspects, especially as he had, long before his death, ceased to find amusement in dissipation, or indeed in the whole range of what is called entertainment—save for his perennial interest in songs. By grace of the radio and of the many musicians who, drawn by his enormous magnetism, made pilgrimages to his bedside, he had a consolation in the last days, and he made the most of it, hilariously rewriting Cole Porter's lyrics in "The New Yorker". But it would be an evasion for the present writer not to say that when he was Ring's neighbour a decade ago, they tucked a lot under their belts in many weathers, and spent many words on many men and things. At no time did I feel that I had known him enough, or that anyone knew him—it was not the feeling that there was more stuff in him and that it should come out, it was rather a qualitative difference, it was rather as though, due to some inadequacy in one's self, one had not penetrated to something unsolved, new and unsaid. That is why one wishes that Ring had written down a large proportion of what was in his mind and heart. It would have saved him longer for us, and that in itself would be something. But I would like to know what it was, and now I will go on wishing—what did Ring want, how did he want things to be, how did he think things were?

A great and good American is dead. Let us not obscure him by the flowers, but walk up and look at that fine medallion, all abraded by sorrows that perhaps we are not equipped to understand. Ring made no enemies, because he was kind, and to many millions he gave release and delight.

Sport and play, by Ring Lardner[2]

Published in Civilization in the United States: An inquiry by thirty Americans (1922)

Bartlett does not tell us who pulled the one about all work and no play, but it probably was the man who said that the longest way round was the shortest way home. There is as much sense in one remark as in the other.

Give me an even start with George M. Cohan, who lives in Great Neck, where I also live, without his suspecting it—give us an even start in the Pennsylvania Station and route me on a Long Island train through Flushing and Bayside while he travels via San Francisco and Yokohama, and I shall undertake to beat him home, even in a blizzard. So much for "the longest way round." Now for the other. If it were your ambition to spend an evening with a dull boy, whom would you choose, H. G. Wells, whose output indicates that he doesn't even take time off to sleep, or the man that closes his desk at two o'clock every afternoon and goes to the ball-game?

---

[2] STEARNS, Harold (Ed.). Civilization in the United States: An inquiry by thirty Americans. United States: Harcourt, Brace and Company, 1922.

You may argue that watching ball-games is not play. It is the American idea of play, which amounts to the same thing, and seventy-five per cent, of the three hundred thousand citizens who do it daily, in season, will tell you seriously that it is all the recreation they get; moreover, that deprived of it, their brain would crack under the strain of "business," that, on account of it, they are able to do more work in the forenoon, and do it better, than would be possible in two or three full days of close sticking on the job. If you believe them, inveterate baseball fans can, in a single morning, dictate as many as four or five twenty-word letters to customers or salesmen, and finish as fresh as a daisy; whereas the non-fan, the grind, is logy and torpid by the time he reaches the second "In reply to same."

But if you won't concede, in the face of the fans' own statement, that it is recreation to look on at baseball or any other sport, then let me ask you to invite to your home some evening, not a mere spectator, but an active participant in any of our popular games—say a champion or near-champion golfer, or a first string pitcher on a big league baseball club. The golfer, let us say, sells insurance half the year and golfs the rest. The pitcher plays eight months of the year and loafs the other four. Bar conversation about their specialty, and you won't find two duller boys than those outside the motion-picture studios.

No, brothers, the bright minds of this or any other country are owned by the men who leave off work only to eat or go to bed. The doodles are the boys who divide their time fifty-fifty between work and play, or who play all the time and don't even pretend to work. Proper exercise undoubtedly promotes good health, but the theory that good health and an active brain are inseparable can be shot full of holes by the mention of two names—Stanislaus Zbyzsk and Robert Louis Stevenson.

It is silly, then, to propound that sport is of mental benefit. Its true, basic function is the cultivation of bodily vigour, with a view to longevity. And longevity, despite the fact that we profess belief in a post-mortem existence that makes this one look sick, is a thing we poignantly desire. Bonehead and wise guy, believer and sceptic—all of us want to postpone as long as possible the promised joy-ride to the Great Beyond. If to participate in sport helps us to do that, then there is good reason to participate in sport.

Well, how many "grown-ups" (normal human beings of twenty-two and under need not be considered; they get all the exercise they require, and then some) in this country, a country that boasts champions in nearly every branch of athletics, derive from play the physical benefit there is in it? What percentage take an active part in what the sporting editors call "the five major sports"—baseball, football, boxing, horse racing, and golf? Let us take them one by one and figure it out, beginning with "the national pastime."

Baseball. Twenty or twenty-one play. Three hundred to forty thousand look on. The latter are, for two hours, "out in the open air," and this, when the air is not so open as to give them pneumonia and when they don't catch something as bad or worse in the street-car or subway train that takes them and brings them back, is a physical benefit. Moreover, the habitual attendant at ball-games is not likely to die of brain fever. But otherwise, the only ones whose health is appreciably promoted are the twenty or twenty-one who play. And they are not doing it for their health.

Football. Thirty play. Thirty thousand look on. One or two of the thirty may be killed or suffer a broken bone, but the general health of the other twenty-nine or twenty-eight is improved by the exercise. As for the thirty thousand, all they get is the open air—usually a little too much of it—and, unless they are hardened to the present-day cheer-leader, a slight feeling of nausea.

Boxing. Eight to ten play. Five thousand to sixty thousand look on. Those of the participants who are masters of defence may profit physically by the training, though the rigorous methods sometimes employed to make an unnatural weight are certainly inimical to health. The ones not expert in defensive boxing, the ones who succeed in the game through their ability to "take punishment" (a trait that usually goes with a low mentality) die, as a rule, before reaching old age, as a result of the "gameness" that made them "successful." There is a limit to the number of punches one can "take" and retain one's health. The five or sixty thousand cannot boast that they even get the air. All but a few of the shows are given indoors, in an atmosphere as fresh and clean as that of the Gopher Prairie day-coach.

Horse Racing. Fifty horses and twenty-five jockeys play. Ten thousand people look on. I can't speak for the horses, but if a jockey wants to remain a jockey, he must, as a rule, eat a great deal less than his little stomach craves, and I don't know of any doctor who prescribes constant underfeeding as conducive to good health in a growing boy.

Racing fans, of course, are out for financial, not physical, gain. They, like the jockeys, are likely to starve to death while still young.

Golf. Here is a pastime in which the players far outnumber the lookers-on. It is a game, if it is a game, that not only takes you out in the open air, but makes you walk, and walking, the doctors say, is all the exercise you need, if you walk five miles or more a day. Golf, then, is really beneficial, and it costs you about $25.00 a week the year round.

So much for our "five major sports." We look on at four of them, and if we can support the family, and pay taxes and insurance, on $1250 a year less than we earn, we take part in the fifth.

The minor sports, as the editor will tell you, are tennis, boating, polo, track athletics, trap-shooting, archery, hockey, soccer, and so on. Not to mention games like poker, bridge, bowling, billiards, and pool (now officially known as "pocket billiards" because the Ladies' Guild thought "pool" must have something to do with betting), which we may dismiss as being of doubtful physical benefit, since they are all played indoors and in a fog of Camel smoke.

Of the outdoor "minors," tennis is unquestionably the most popular. And it is one whale of a game—if you can stand it. But what percentage of grown-ups play it? I have no statistics at hand, and must guess. The number of adult persons with whom I am acquainted, intimately or casually, is possibly two thousand. I can think of ten who play as many as five sets of tennis a year.

How many of the two thousand play polo or have ever played polo? One. How many are trap-shooters? Two. How many have boats? Six or seven. How many run footraces or jump? None. How many are archers? None. How many play hockey, soccer, la crosse? None.

If I felt like indulging in a game of cricket, which God forbid, whom should I call up and invite to join me?

Now, how many of my two thousand acquaintances are occasional or habitual spectators at baseball games, football games, boxing matches, or horse races? All but three or four. The people I know (I do not include ball-players, boxers, and wrestlers, who make their living from sport) are average people; they are the people you know. And the overwhelming majority of them don't play.

Why not? If regular participation in a more or less interesting outdoor game is going to lengthen our lives, why don't we participate? Is it because we haven't time? It takes just as much time to look on, and we do that. Is it because we can't afford it? We can play tennis for as little as it costs to go to the bail-game and infinitely less than it costs to go to the races.

We don't play because (1) we lack imagination, and because (2) we are a nation of hero-worshippers.

When we were kids, the nurse and the minister taught us that, if we weren't good, our next stop would be hell. But, to us, there was no chance of the train's starting for seventy years. And we couldn't visualize an infernal excursion that far off. It was too vague to be scary. We kept right on swiping the old man's cigars and giggling in the choir. If they had said that misdemeanours such as those would spell death and eternal fire, not when we were old, but to-morrow, most of us would have respected father's property rights and sat through the service with a sour pan. If the family doctor were to tell us now that unless we got outdoors and exercised every afternoon this week, we should die next Tuesday before lunch, you can bet we should get outdoors and exercise every afternoon this week. But when he tells us that, without healthful outdoor sport, we shall die in 1945 instead of 1949, why, it doesn't mean anything. It's a chimera, a myth, like the next war.

But hero-worship is the national disease that does most to keep the grandstands full and the playgrounds empty. To hell with those four extra years of life, if they are going to cut in on our afternoon at the Polo Grounds, where, in blissful asininity, we may feast our eyes on the swarthy Champion of Swat, shouting now and then in an excess of anile idolatry, "Come on, you Babe. Come on, you Baby Doll!" And if an hour of tennis is going to make us late at the Garden, perhaps keep us out of our ringside seats, so close to Dempsey's corner that (O bounteous God!) a drop of the divine perspiration may splash our undeserving snout—Hang up, liver! You're on a busy wire!

Discover Tacet Books

We are an independent publishing house that publishes interesting and unique works by classic authors—in their original languages—at affordable prices for readers. Our catalog features works in English, Spanish, and Portuguese by great authors such as James Joyce, Virginia Woolf, Machado de Assis, George Orwell, Horacio Quiroga, and more. We offer unique collections such as Feminist Fiction, Victorian Fairy Tales, and selections of short stories from countries like Cuba, Spain, Argentina, and Mexico, among others.

Whether you're studying a new language or enjoying classics in their original languages, our books will make an excellent addition to your library.

Visit our website: **www.tacetbooks.com**

www.tacetbooks.com

www.ingramcontent.com/pod-product-compliance
Lightning Source LLC
LaVergne TN
LVHW040046080526
838202LV00045B/3519